The Janet Network

The Janet Network

By:

MICHELE WALLACE CAMPANELLI

ARPress
45 Dan Road Suite 5
Canton MA 02021

Hotline: 1(888) 821-0229
Fax: 1(508) 545-7580

Ordering Information:
Quantity sales. Special discounts are available on quantity purchases by corporations, associations, and others. For details, contact the publisher at the address above.

Printed in the United States of America.

ISBN-13: Softcover   979-8-89330-170-0
           eBook   979-8-89330-171-7
           Hardcover   979-8-89330-172-4

Library of Congress Control Number: 2024902554

Dedication

This book is written in honor of:

The Woman's Center of Melbourne, Serene Harbor and Project Response and Susan G. Komen Breast Cancer Foundation.

I would like to thank God, my wonderful late husband Louis V. Campanelli III, my brother David & Greg, Dawn & Ben Kreiselman, the entire Wallace & Campanelli family, St. Marks United Methodist Church & Choir, Sherry MacLean, Space Coast Symphony Orchestra, Brevard Symphony Orchestra, Brevard Cultural Alliance, Seeta Media Inc. & WMELradio, Melisa & Dick, St. Mark's UMC, Eastern Florida State College for the Music Scholarship, KeriAnne N. Burgin, Jackie Hitzig, Steve & Heather Sigety, in honor of Kristen, Amanda, and those with breast cancer, Marsha Briscoe, Melanie Billings, Debra and Steven Womack, Brook D. Goldfarb, Kim Perry, Jill Carlyle, the Florida PD, FBI and DEA for keeping drugs off out streets.

A special thanks goes to my mother and editor, Fontaine M. Wallace, who raised me to be imaginative and believe in my talents. There were several women and a special physiatrist who were muses for this fiction book. They will remain nameless but know that you will be forever in my prayers and considered my dear friends. Thank you for the inspiration.

To God be the Glory!

I alone know the plans I have for you, plans to bring you prosperity and not disaster, plans to bring about the future you hope for.

Jeremiah 29:11

Contents

CHAPTER 1

Tears streamed down her mother Marla's pudgy cheeks, so Catherine reached out and embraced her as tightly as she could. Trying to calm her nervous reaction, Catherine sputtered, "We'll make it through this."

"Of course; I'm worried about the cancer, but most of all…" her mother intoned, releasing her daughter from the grasp. Her mother stood, straightening her T-shirt over her jeans. "Most of all, I'm worried about you."

"Doctor Burrows said they caught your breast lump in time. I'll be right there at the hospital with you for the operation and I'm sure Lucky won't mind if I give you a ride to treatment." Catherine tried to keep her voice steady.

"You don't understand." Her mother wiped her eyes. "I'm not that worried about my diagnosis!"

Catherine shrugged her shoulders. "Then what's wrong? Isn't the latest mammogram why you're so upset, Mom?"

"Oh, I should have taken better care of myself," she announced. "Eaten more vegetables. Drunk more water. Stayed out of the sun in the summer. There's so much that I would change now."

"Mom, stop blaming yourself!"

"How can I not?"

"We don't know what caused your cancer!" Catherine reassured. "Didn't Great Aunt Eloise have it?"

"Your father should have been around for us more. He wasn't a good role model," the mother added more softly. "First, he cheated on me with Carol Ann Montgomery, the paralegal. That was hard enough to take, especially because she was such a whore who had slept with two other lawyers at his firm. I asked him to stay, go into marriage counseling, and we'd try to work out our problems. When he told me he was leaving for that bimbo, I nearly had a nervous breakdown. I could have dealt with losing him though. What really got to me is after we had that horrible divorce in which I got absolutely nothing thanks to his law firm…when he finally did come around for his weekends with you, he never gave you the attention you deserved. He spent all his time, answering business phone calls or setting up meetings with clients for his firm. He hardly spoke to me; he didn't do the normal things Dads do with their daughters. I wish he would have taken you out for pizza, movies or even one of his baseball games. You would have enjoyed those things. You were just a teenager who needed her father."

"He had two other children with his new wife Carol. I understood."

"Don't call her that! Don't ever call her that."

"Yes, Mom, I meant to say he had other children with that woman you hate so much."

"I didn't see this coming." Her mother plopped on the recliner and struggled to quit sniffling.

"What are you talking about?" Catherine asked, anxiously. "Mom, I realize we got horrific news today, but you aren't making any sense. Whatever you need, I'll be there for you. I'll go to the operation. I'll cook, clean, whatever you ask for while you recover, okay?"

"Listen." Her mother held up a hand. "Just listen to me for one moment. I know it isn't my place but I have to get this off my chest."

"The operation will remove the lump. Doctor Burrows sounded as if he was sure we caught the cancer early enough."

"Will you please shut up?" Her mother's voice tremored as if talking to a child who had just gotten in trouble, not the mid-thirties woman she had grown into. "I need to say this or I'll never forgive myself! Now listen."

Catherine sat back and took a deep breath. "What is it? Is there more that you aren't telling me?"

"Yes, but not about my health. When you get to be sixty-five years old and facing what possibly could be a fatal disease…"

"It's not!" Catherine angrily disagreed. "The doctor said that he felt that he could get it all with one operation!"

"Chances are I will be one of those millions of breast cancer survivors that you hear about, but there is still that chance that I won't be." Her mother struggled to maintain a smile. "If I'm not. If I shouldn't make it, I can't hold my tongue any longer. I have to tell you how I feel. As your mother, I've really tried to stay out of your personal life. Now I realize that it might have been a mistake since I might not have all the time in the world."

"I don't understand."

Marla reached out and patted Catherine's knee. "I love you."

"I love you, too, Mom. I don't want you to think for one moment that you weren't a great Mom."

Her mother gulped. "I did the best I could which apparently wasn't enough."

"I wouldn't want any other mother in the whole world," Catherine said and gasped. "Now please, let's go out for dinner and try not to let this get us down. Your operation isn't for two more weeks."

"This has nothing to do with my going under the knife." Quietly her mother reached into her jean pocket and pulled out a business card.

Catherine read the name Janet Keller, Mental Health Counselor. "Mom, if you want to go to counseling over divorcing Dad or having breast cancer, I support you."

"Not me." Her mother gulped hard. "You, Dear."

"Me?" Catherine gasped. "For what?"

"For Lucky," her mother responded.

"My boyfriend?"

"I can't leave this earth knowing that you won't be taken care of. He's wrong for you!"

"But we love each other!" Catherine's voice rose in pitch.

"He's abusive," Marla countered more quietly.

Catherine stood, putting her hands defensively on her hips. "Lucky takes great care of me."

Her mother rose, too, and wrapped an arm around Catherine's shoulder. "How many times have I heard him put you down or insult you in public? He doesn't treat you the way you deserve."

"Come on." Catherine laughed, nervously. "It's not that bad."

"I've seen your bruises. Don't lie to me. I know that son-of-a-bitch put them on you!"

"Mom!" Catherine pulled away. "Don't talk about Lucky that way."

"I can't stay silent anymore! If I die, he's the last man on earth I want to see you married to! Don't let him control your life anymore. He's too violent. You can do better! I know you can do better."

"This is none of your concern. We should be concentrating on you right now."

Her mother wiped her eyes and closed the gap between them. "I want only the best for you. Lucky isn't the one. I'm sorry if this hurts your feelings, but I want you to go to a counselor and rethink about answering yes when he asks you to marry him."

"First of all, he's only hinted around about us someday getting married. I can't believe you're this upset over just the possibility."

"Go to Counselor Janet. She came highly recommended by my friend at work. She supposedly is the best person in town for relationship problems."

"I love Lucky," Catherine protested, shaking her head.

Her mother nodded back no. "How can you love someone who keeps raising a hand against you? Do you think that's what God wants for you? I want you to consider counseling."

"I won't go." Catherine pushed the card back to her mother.

"Promise me, you'll keep the card."

"Mom, I won't hear any more bad talk about Lucky." Catherine stomped a foot.

Her mother backed away. "I wiped your cute little baby butt… Keep that card. It's the least you can do for me!"

"Fine." Catherine stuffed the card in her purse. "But I'm not going. I can promise you that."

CHAPTER 2

Sitting at a candlelit table, Lucky removed his folded napkin from his china plate and unfolded it carefully on his lap. At the same time, Catherine checked her diamond watch; she had arrived at the restaurant to meet him five minutes late.

She knew he'd be angry.

Quickly, she slipped past the couples waiting to be seated and hurried to the table to join a very tall, dark, handsome man in a dashing black suit. Many of the women around him stared at him. Lucky's full lips curved into a smile when he saw Catherine approaching.

"Sorry, I'm late," she apologized.

"Traffic?" Lucky questioned, rising to kiss her on the cheek and push her chair away from the table.

"Yes," she admitted, immediately sitting down. "There was an accident on Tenth Avenue and the police had one lane blocked."

"I don't like to wait."

"I know," she murmured.

"Chicken al'orange is a specialty of Leon's. I ordered it especially for you."

"Thank you. You're so thoughtful."

"So, what did you do today?" He replaced the napkin on his lap and picked up a glass of wine. "I called our house twice and no one answered."

"My mother got some bad news. She tested positive and she'll be having an operation in a few weeks," Catherine replied softly with downcast eyes.

"It's breast cancer, then?" He raised the glass to his lips and drank slowly.

"She was very upset. I stayed most of the afternoon."

"Without calling?" he snapped. "You didn't answer your cell phone either."

"I turned it off while we were in the doctor's office. I didn't want to interrupt my mother's meeting with him. I'm sorry."

As he lowered his glass, his smile disappeared. "I don't expect that to happen again. I want to get a hold of you when I need to; I wanted to invite you to Leon's."

"I got your message when I got home." Catherine grinned. "I made it."

"Not on time," he said and scoffed.

"Sorry."

Just then a waitress placed a basket of crackers and brie in the middle of the table, filled Catherine's glass with water, and asked, "Would you like a glass of champagne or the house specialty wine?"

"She won't be having any alcohol tonight," Lucky answered for her. Catherine smiled at the waitress. She had wanted a small sip of the wine Lucky was drinking, but decided it was better not to argue with him while he was in such a foul mood.

"You can drive. I'm in the mood to drink tonight."

Catherine glanced around the upscale restaurant with its seaside oil paintings and indirect lighting. "This is nice," she added to soften his anger.

"You're not dressed appropriately. That gown is too low cut," he commented, pointing briefly at her bosom.

She immediately looked down at the neckline which plummeted down her cleavage. "Remember when you took me to Quincy Marcos and picked this dress out for me."

"I'd never pick anything so tasteless," he rebuffed. Catherine glanced at the floor to avoid his denial.

"That should be in a tramp's wardrobe or thrown out," he sputtered in disgust.

She loved what she was wearing, the feel of the black satin against her skin and the lace at the hem. "You're right. It is too tight and low. I'll toss it in the garbage when we get home."

"Stop wasting my money, Catherine, with your bad taste."

"I'll be more careful." Suddenly having the urge to eat half the plate and stuff emotions, Catherine reached for a cracker. After spreading the slightly salty cheese, then adding the sweet chutney, she enjoyed the moment of the tasty treasure.

"Not too much." He pulled the appetizer plate closer to him. "You've already gained too much weight since Christmas. You need to watch your carbs if you are going to lose it before summer."

"Of course."

"You want to wear a bathing suit again, right?" he questioned.

"I love spending time in our pool since you added the fountain."

"That's right." He winked. "You look better with a tan."

"My goal is to lose twenty pounds by June."

"Not by eating like a pig," Lucky added.

"You'll enjoy the crackers," she added. "They make them, fresh."

Lucky began to chew slowly. "Chef Leon is from the islands; I flew a whole group of his friends in from the Bahamas."

"That must have been an interesting flight."

"Leon assured me that they would be renting more jets in the future. Of course, they want Busi-jet's food to improve."

"Kat's not warming up the meatloaf, right?" Catherine joked.

Ignoring her humorous comment, he gulped down more wine. "By the way, I'm going to be flying some tourists to Mexico. I'll be back on Friday, perhaps by nightfall."

Catherine was thankful. "That will give me plenty of time to spend with my mother then."

Lucky took another cheese covered cracker and continued to munch. "I think your mother needs some time to accept her situation. It would be better if you stayed at the house in case the Millers stop by. I'm expecting some news on refinancing Busi-jet and their possibly purchasing more planes for the company."

"But what can I do?"

"Just be home in case they drop by with papers," Lucky ordered, coldly. "The Millers could be very important to Busi-jet. I may sell part of my ownership of Busi-jet if we can come to an arrangement that suits both parties. That could mean dozens of high-class clients."

"You keep reminding me of how wonderful those Millers are." Catherine could barely believe he came up with such an excuse to keep her away from her mom. "I do need to spend time with my mother though."

He leaned over the table and grabbed her wrist. Slowly, his fingers tightened until she grimaced in pain. "Did you not hear me?" His tone threatened.

"Uh-huh," she muttered.

"What did you say? I didn't hear you."

Her eyes lowered to her black shoes. "Yes." She noticed a dirt spot on the left corner of her right foot, above her big toe. For a moment, she wondered where she'd gotten it, trying not to think of the agony he was causing to her wrist. When he let go, she reached down into her purse to pull out a tissue. Her fingers fumbled through the lipstick and compact mirror. In between her index and thumb, she felt the card her mother had just given her hours before.

"This could mean many more scheduled flights, a real coup for the company."

"Excuse me." Catherine tried to pull her hand from his grasp. "I need to use the restroom."

He released her and then added sarcastically, "By all means. I would hate for you to ruin that dress."

She rose from the table and strode toward the back of the restaurant. Her mother had Lucky pegged as an abuser even though Catherine had tried to keep it from her. She had thought she did a good job, until today. "I've wanted to leave him for a long time, Mom," she mumbled to herself. "But how?"

CHAPTER 3

The psychiatrist straightened his spectacles, opened his office door and strode to his plush chair behind a long, mahogany desk. What was waiting across the small room on a small settee, he didn't expect. He guessed this beautiful woman's age around his and noticed the way she studied him. Her eyes were observing his crew cut, gray-blond hair and his gentle features. She was finding him like most women did, appealing.

"Good morning. You are Catherine Walters?" He reached out and firmly shook her hand.

"Yes."

"Do you like to be called Cathy," he began reviewing her file, "or Catherine?"

"Whatever you prefer." She gulped.

He noticed her hands shaking. "Nervous?"

"A bit," she admitted.

"Is that the reason you came to visit me today? Are you having problems with anxiety?" he inquired.

For a moment, she seemed to forget why she had come and kept staring at him. Speechless, he smiled at her silence. The captivation woman looking at him usually disappeared after a few initial visits. He too took the time to study her. Catherine was slightly overweight, but all extremities seemed to be in working order. Her long brunette hair and grayish-blue eyes presented a stunning picture. He guessed most men would find her attractive.

"Are you having a problem staying focused?" was his next question.

"You are so young. Are you Doctor Newport?"

"Yes, Newport and I'm in my forties. I just got your records from your family physician, and I have to say there is no mention of any previous mental conditions. I'm a bit curious as to why you are here."

"I was recommended by a friend of my mother's. She suggested that I make an appointment with Janet."

"Janet." His eyes tightened.

"Is Janet another Doctor here?"

"She's gone from our medical practice now," he announced.

"Originally, I made my appointment with her and then got a call back from your office that you were the one taking on her clients."

"Patients," he corrected, leaning back in his chair. "I'm glad you came then. So, are you having problems with your spouse or boyfriend?"

"Why do you ask?"

"Janet's specialty is," the doctor explained, "couples and relationship counseling."

Catherine understood. "I see why Janet was suggested then."

The Doctor took out a pen and clicked it several times. "Why don't we start with twenty easy questions? That always seems to work for me getting to know a new patient."

Catherine fidgeted in the chair across from him, crossing her legs. Her brows were raised as she waited for his first question.

"Are you in a troubled relationship?"

"Define trouble." Catherine breathed deeply.

"You are a teacher of some kind? Yes, a Teaching Assistant for the sixth grade." He continued scanning through her file. "No children of your own though I see. You're not married. And you are how old?"

"Are you trying to make me feel bad enough, so I'll need medication?" Catherine joked.

He grinned again, flipping to the next page. "There's nothing here about your sexual preference. Is your partner a man or a woman?"

"Do I look butch?"

"There isn't a look for that sort of thing," he said and chuckled. "I assure you it's merely a sexual orientation question."

"Yes, I do believe I see your point. You are just asking to see what my problem relationship is."

He quickly added, "Or you could just come right out and tell me why you feel you need counseling or medication."

"This isn't easy opening up to a stranger."

"Then picture me as someone you like to converse with," he suggested. "Whatever is happening in your current relationship, it's upsetting you?"

"My boyfriend Lucky is becoming more and more violent toward me." Catherine sighed. "I really hate to admit that. He's a pilot. He owns Busi-Jet, a jet company which provides service to wealthy businessmen who need to get to meetings all over the southern states and the Bahamas."

"Sounds exciting. A pilot."

"He's gone most of the time which helps," Catherine said.

"You want out of the relationship?" he asked.

"I tried to leave him last month. I packed my things and moved back to a friend's house in Orlando. Within two days he found me and talked me into coming back. When I got home, he beat me up so badly I couldn't leave the house for a week. I lost that Teaching Assistant job because of it."

The doctor spent a few minutes writing information into her file. "Are you having problems sleeping?"

"I'm nervous all the time. I'm wondering when it will happen again."

"So, you are still with him?"

She fought back tears. "Is there something you can give me for the nerves? My mother used to take Valium. She's dealing with a lot right now and that's also upsetting me."

"There are newer drugs," the Doctor announced. "I have some samples of the latest anti-anxiety medication."

"Whatever you feel is best." Her eyes spilled tears.

"Can I hold you to that?" He opened up a desk drawer and then handed her a small box of samples.

"What do you mean?"

"I want you to come back next week, Catherine. Let me know how this medication works for you and we'll talk further about the person you are in a relationship with." He handed her a tissue and stood. "There could be a few side effects, so I want you to take notes if you have any problems. If the medication isn't something you can handle, I want you to call me immediately, and I'll write another prescription."

"Okay."

"Don't be discouraged if this one doesn't work. There are many different types of anti-anxiety medications, and it may just take several visits to find you the right one which works best for you."

"You are very kind," she murmured.

"I hope in time you'll feel that it is easier to open up to me. Try not to think of me as a stranger but someone here to help you."

"I appreciate your listening."

"It's why I'm here." He shook her hand goodbye.

Suddenly, she turned back around and looked him right in the eye. "Doctor?"

"You can call me Jay."

"For some reason I prefer calling you by your title, Doctor, if you don't mind. Would that be fine?"

"Doc it is." He smiled. "Is there something else?"

"What I told you about my boyfriend Lucky remains a secret, right? I don't want my problems to get out."

He released her hand. "My office is like Vegas: what happens here remains completely confidential."

"Thank you," she said, heading out of his office. "I'll see you next week."

He noticed the way she moved with a slight sashay in her stride, caused by her three-inch heels clicking against the hard wood of his office floor. He slowly closed her file just as she shut the door. "Looking forward to it."

CHAPTER 4

The moment Catherine left his office, the doctor fumbled through his top desk drawer and pulled out a handheld multimedia phone device. He used his stylus to click on the letter P of the address book, opening PRIVATE INVESTIGATIONS, Will Cilva Ltd. Quickly, he pulled off a wireless headset from the side and clicked on the talk button.

He heard three rings before a woman answered, "Cilva Investigations. How may I direct your call?"

"Will, please. It's Jay."

"Good morning, Dr. Newport," she replied, overly friendly. "How are you today?"

"I'm well, Beatrice."

"This is a pleasant surprise. I'm going to that diner for lunch in an hour. I'd love to treat you if you aren't too swamped with patients." She sounded almost desperate.

"My plate's full today," he said, turning her down gently.

"You've got a rain check," she said. "I'll put you right through."

"Thank you, Beatrice. Have a nice day."

"Of course, Doctor Newport."

There were a few clicks, followed by soft sounding music, and then a boisterous voice boomed, "Jay! What's up, Buddy?"

"I took over another patient for Janet," the doctor announced.

"You want a full investigation." Will understood.

"She's being abused by a pilot." The doctor glanced out the window, turning his chair to look at the pond. A white egret was scooping up minnows with its long, thin bill by the water's edge. "Ever heard of…" He reopened Catherine's file on his lap. "Busi-jet?"

"That's a privately owned airport on the west side. It's a small strip with a few high-class planes," Will announced. "I've done some investigations near there. Upscale clientele from what I could see."

"I'm concerned about this patient's present safety level."

He immediately questioned. "Is she trustworthy?"

"Keep this as hush as possible seeing the position I'm in."

"No need to explain." "So, what's the creep's name?"

"I'm not sure if you should just investigate him or her too," the doctor said and sighed. "It may be best if we keep an eye on both. Do you have the manpower?"

"Fred. And I'm interviewing someone who worked for Blackwell this afternoon, Blake."

The egret outside his window began to unfold its wings to warm himself in the sun. The doctor took a moment to glance over to an empty bird feeder by his window and another bird, a bright, red male cardinal, waited nearby on a rock. He opened the bottom drawer of his desk and discovered that he was out of birdseed.

"Jay, you want the whole caboodle?"

"I want to see what pans out in the original run. Her name is Catherine Walter. Boyfriend's name is…" He rechecks the file. "Lucky. Looks like all I've got is a nickname."

"It could be legal. I met a Lucky once in Nevada."

"Can't tell you, Will," the doctor admitted.

"And you're sure he works for this Busi-jet company?"

"Catherine claims she wants to leave the pilot. I need to know more."

"Is it physical or mental abuse?"

"Both, I believe," he said and sighed. "He apparently isn't letting her go but travels often which leaves some room to wonder why she hasn't gone while he's out of town. I'm guessing he must be very violent and threatening her regularly. I'll need to know his piloting schedule."

"That's the first thing I'll uncover," Will said. "How much do you want to spend here… 24-hour surveillance on Lucky with a bodyguard following Catherine? How do you want us to work it this time?"

"I have a new idea with this case. We may need to create a whole team." Will wondered.

"Let me guess. You want to get involved too?"

"You know me," he said and chuckled softly.

"What's she like?"

"I always say the best-looking ones are with the worst men in town," the doctor said.

"That's one mystery I have yet to solve." Will laughed. "Let me check to see if Fred's available to start right away." Silence prevailed while the doctor continued to watch the egret step gingerly across the edge of the pond. Several frogs hopped out of his way to protect themselves from being eaten.

"I'll be sure to discount 25% off our normal daily fee for Fred's coverage."

"I think I would prefer your protecting her too," Doctor Newport finally decided.

"Really?"

"This may be a more serious case." There was a pause.

"I can't wait to hear what you want me to do, Jay. We haven't worked a case together since that redhead, Lynn."

The door opened with a tall, thin, middle-aged woman quickly placing a file on the doctor's desk. "Edward Martins," she announced.

In walked the next patient, an older man, who hunched over as he tapped his cane in step before reaching the sofa. After resting his cane on the side, he leaned his body as far back as he could.

"Good morning, Edward," the doctor greeted. "How are you?"

"Better, Doctor."

"I'll be right with you. I'll only be one more minute."

"Take your time," Edward mumbled.

"Will, I'd like to take a trip to South Beach this weekend. Perhaps we could check out a few clubs," he said into the thin multimedia phone's headset. "Why don't you see if that private jet company can fly us down there? I'm not on call this weekend at the hospital, so I could leave after five on Friday and not need to come back until late Sunday night."

"When do you see Catherine again?"

The doctor checked on his desktop computer to see when she was scheduled. "Margie just put her in for Tuesday morning. So let's get this planned for this weekend if you can book a flight."

"I'll schedule Fred on her while we're gone. I may be hiring that new employee with a great deal of surveillance experience. We'll see how Blake Anderson fits into our team when I get to know him better."

"Good man."

"Don't worry, Jay. It's the least I can do for Janet," Will said. "Who knows if I'll meet a new girlfriend in South Beach, I'll be sure to give you an extra discount for time getting off."

The doctor laughed. "Thanks, Will."

"Always a pleasure."

The doctor disconnected the phone, then turned the chair around to find his patient sleeping. A short snort escaped his lips before the doctor suddenly made a loud coughing noise to wake him up.

"Oh, sorry, Doctor," he said and yawned.

"That's quite all right, Edward."

"I've been very sleepy in the mornings," he informed the doctor.

"That is one of the side effects of your new prescription. Why don't we lessen the dosage and see if that doesn't work better."

CHAPTER 5

Will pulled his black pickup truck into the lot of the giant outdoor skate park. He parked the vehicle right in front of the open gate, and noticed the young man seated on a wooden bench. His hand grasped a skateboard with a smiling yellow skull on the front. Dressing as he appeared on television, Blake sported jean shorts, a white muscle tank, and long blond hair pulled back into a ponytail.

"What's up?" Will heard as he climbed down from the cab.

"Blake Anderson?" Will acknowledged his identity but wanted verification.

"In the flesh," he said, planted the board and stood and extended his hand. "You must be Will Cilva, Private Investigations, right?"

Will nodded.

"Blackwell told me all about your company," Blake acknowledged, sitting back down. "He said now that I've moved down here from New Jersey, you were the man to see in the area if I wanted to continue spying."

"Being a Private Investigator," Will corrected.

"Same thing."

Will watched the young men skating in the park for a moment and then sat down on the bench, which then squeaked.

"What kind of hours are you offering?" Blake inquired.

"First of all, I spoke to Blakewell and you came highly recommended. In fact, you almost sounded too good to be true." Will breathed deeply. "He said you are relentless in pursuit."

"I've never lost a client," Blake bragged.

"Total any cars?"

Blake's smile dropped. "Wow, you know the right question to ask, don't you? Is that going to be a problem?"

"Chances are you will be teamed with Fred for a while so I don't think you'll be driving," Will explained. "I want to make sure you know how I run things before I put you on your own surveillance assignments."

"Who's Fred?"

"Fred is an employee who has worked for me for many years. You'll like him. He's got a great eye."

Blake picked up his board, took a hand towel from his back pocket and began to wipe it clean. "I'm sure Blackwell told you that hiring me would be the best decision you could make."

Blake was young and it showed in his tough attitude. Even with an ego bigger than life, Blake still seemed reliable and reportedly had helped solve over 1/3 of Blackwell's cases. Blake's greatest assets, according to Blakewell, were that Blake was fast on his feet and not afraid of knocking a man's block off. Besides training in kick boxing, Blake also knew how to shoot a gun since his father was a NYPD officer and had taken him hunting. "I have to admit your last boss told me he was sorry you quit."

Blake confessed, "My old lady got a job in Florida."

"Your mother and father got divorced?"

"No, my girl came to Florida to go to college. She was tired of the snow and talked me into it so that I could skate and surf year round," Blake added. "I'll miss New Jersey and my winters in Hawaii but I'd miss my girlfriend more."

"She must really be something."

Blake pulled out his wallet and opened it up to show a picture of a blonde female wearing a string bikini. "You'd pack for her, too. Her name's Candy and sweet doesn't even cover it."

Will laughed. "Candy's a bit young for me."

"She's twenty-one but acts like my mom when I stay out too late in the clubs."

"So you've worked for Blackwell since you graduated from high school?" Will inquired. "How long in the field?"

"Three years and five months." Blake sighed. "He was a cool boss. We made lots of busts and helped out parole officers and sometimes even bounty hunters. My favorite case was when I caught this millionaire cheating on his wife. I got footage of him and his mistress on the balcony. The tape wound up in the divorce proceedings."

"So you know that many of our cases are private matters?"

"Of course." Blake smiled. "Blackwell worked a lot with police officers too."

"You won't work with the cops in my organization." Will grimaced. "I've burnt a few bridges in that area."

Blake finished wiping his board and plunked it down on the ground. "So how many hours? Candy's into upgrades and I need to be rollin'."

"I'm offering over forty a week especially now that I'm starting a new case. Do you have a problem signing a confidentiality agreement for keeping our clients information privileged?"

Blake admitted, "Blackwell made me sign a new contract every year."

"Good." Will glanced back over his shoulder to the skaters. "My only concern on hiring you is that people might recognize you."

"I've only won a few skating competitions." Blake shrugged. "I'm not Tony Hawk famous… yet. There is a contest coming up next month at the Skateway-X Games that I agreed to appear at. That's the only day I know I can't work."

"Do people come up to you and ask for autographs?"

"Rarely. I wear a helmet and a clear mask. Most people don't know who I am; it's my board if anything some recognize." He pointed to the skull smiley face. "Or if I wear a shirt with this symbol on it."

Will made his decision. "We've got a really important case we need some extra hands on. Come to the office tomorrow and sign the contract. We pay per hour and offer bonus opportunities as well. Hopefully, you'll feel comfortable since I run a tight ship just like Blackwell."

"You and Blackwell close?" Blake asked.

"Blackwell is my cousin," Will confessed. "He taught me how to be a Private Investigator. If you know how he runs things, you should do fine working for me. Just keep a low profile and we'll have no problems. Although, you might want to consider cutting your hair."

"Either you take me with the hair or it's a no go." Will laughed.

"It makes you stand out."

Blake stood up, grabbed his board and headed for the gate to enter the park. "I'll stop by your office tomorrow to sign my life away but not my hair. Okay, dude?"

Will chuckled as he rose. Blake had exactly the attitude necessary to be a great investigator, fearlessness. Like all the great investigators before him, Blake beat to his own drummer.

"Okay… dude."

CHAPTER 6

Catherine wasn't expecting her mother at the door but was very pleased that she had stopped by. Thankful that Lucky had left for his trip to Mexico, she welcomed her in. "Mom, why didn't you call?"

"I've been waiting for you." Her mother pushed in and looked around. "Is he here? Is that why you haven't dropped by?"

"No, Lucky's gone until Friday. I've just been really busy," Catherine lied. "I'm sorry I didn't call."

"I had hoped that we could spend some time together," her mother suggested. "Why don't we go to a movie or hit the mall?"

Catherine remembered how Lucky wanted her to stay home. "I have so much to do this afternoon. Why don't we see a movie next week?"

Her mother frowned in disappointment. Then she moved past Catherine toward the glass doors that led out to the pool. "Then why don't I just stay here and go for a swim?"

Catherine immediately agreed. "I have an old bathing suit that should fit you."

"If this is the way it has to be." Her mother turned her back.

"What do you mean, Mom?"

"He told you not to spend time with me. Didn't he?" her mother guessed. "That's just the type of guy he is, keeping you isolated from your family and friends."

"I have no friends, Mom." Catherine headed to the stairs toward the bedroom to retrieve the suit for her mother. "You make it sound like all my problems are Lucky's fault."

"You lost some friends because of the Christmas party when he got drunk and insulted half of the guests," her mother pressed. "Lucky has a way of making people feel very intimidated. It serves a purpose for him. The fewer people around, the more he can control your every action."

Catherine turned on a heel and faced her mother. "If all you are going to do is talk bad about Lucky, then maybe you'd better go."

Her mother sighed. "Fine. I'll behave."

"Lucky called this morning and let me know that he has another trip to Miami and wants me to meet him in South Beach."

Her mother huffed. "He's sending the Busi-jet company car, right?"

"Yes, Mom." Catherine smiled.

"Of course. He would never want you to drive yourself anywhere."

Catherine rushed up the stairs to get two bathing suits and some towels; she didn't want to be reminded of how controlled her life had become. Should she even tell her mother that she called the number for Janet? What if she changed her mind and wanted to stay with Lucky? Besides, she ended up getting Doctor Newport instead of Janet. Her mother would probably complain that she had gone to the wrong person.

When Catherine reached the bottom of the stairs, her mother was sitting at the dining room table, her head clasped in her hands. "Mom?" Aware her mother was crying, Catherine dropped the garments and hurried over. "Are you okay?"

"I'm so scared," her mother admitted. "I don't want cancer. Why did this happen to me?"

Catherine placed her hand on her shoulder.

Her mother wiped her eyes and tapped Catherine's hand. "Just knowing that I can see you when I'm down… it makes a difference."

"I'm so sorry this is happening to you, Mom."

"I need to keep the attitude that I can beat this. If I can survive your father leaving, then I can handle this operation and possible chemo if the doctor can't get all of the cancer." She didn't quite sound sure of herself, however.

Catherine slowly began to rub her mother's shoulders. "I have some news," Catherine decided to tell her. "I called the number on the card."

Her mother's eyes widened with glee. "And what did Janet say?"

"Janet apparently has left the practice but I did see someone else, Doctor Jay Newport."

"Newport? My friend from work didn't mention a Newport, only that Janet was considered the best in her field," her mother retorted. "What was this Doctor Newport like?"

"Handsome," Catherine smiled, "and knowledgeable. The visit really seemed to help, so I think I'll see him again."

"Handsome?" Her mother grinned.

"Don't worry, Mom. I'm not his type. Not many men are going for overweight and crazy. He did help though."

"He diagnosed you crazy?"

"No," Catherine added. "In fact, he seemed to be very understanding. I'm glad that I was assigned him instead of Janet. At first I wasn't sure I could open up to a stranger, but Dr. Newport was very friendly. After a while I felt comfortable."

"I'm so glad!" Her mother jumped up and embraced Catherine. "This is an answer to my prayers."

"I'm not sure I'll ever leave Lucky, Mom," Catherine declared.

Her mother released her. "It just makes me feel better, okay, to know that you are talking to someone. Did you bring up your father?"

Catherine grimaced. "I really don't think he has anything to do with the fact that Lucky has some control problems."

Her mother's hands grabbed Catherine's cheeks and squeezed. "This is the first step!"

"Mom, you really are expecting a lot from one doctor's visit. I just went, told him a little of what's going on, and he prescribed some anxiety medication that might help me deal with things."

"I have been so concerned about your stress." Her mother's face was beaming with gladness.

"Are you ready to swim then?"

Her mother shook her head no. "I just would rather have some lunch and keep talking. Would that be all right?"

"I've got chicken salad in the fridge."

"Let's order a pizza." Her mother grinned. "This is turning out to be a celebration, a pizza kind of day!"

CHAPTER 7

The front door to the office building banged open and in strolled Blake Anderson carrying a surfboard and sporting nothing more than a pair of swim trunks and flip-flops. Tracy, Will's full-time secretary, gasped at the very sight of the magnificent surfer. She rose to her feet with her eyes glued to Blake's muscular, tan chest.

"Blake Anderson!" Tracy rose from her chair to give him a high-five. "Is that you? I'm such a fan!"

Blake placed the surfboard on the beige, leather sofa and grinned as he high-fived her. "Will Cilva in?"

"Welcome to Cilva Investigations," Tracy greeted. "It's such an honor to be working with you. I saw you win the gold in the Game BMX in Hawaii. You were so awesome!"

Blake cocked his head and winked. "Wait till the Skateway-X Games. I've got a whole new bag of tricks."

"You're not worried about Ray Clifford then?"

"Ray's got nothing on me."

Tracy's blue eyes fixated on Blake. Her smile brightened. She flipped her long, brown hair over one shoulder and sat back down behind the polished desk. "I'll tell Mr. Cilva that you are here, Blake."

"Thanks, sweetheart." Then he held up a hand. "Sorry, I have to remember I'm not back in Jersey. I meant to say, thank you, Miss. I tend to be a bit informal where I work."

"You can call me sweetheart or anything you like."

"What's your real name?"

"Tracy Evans and I'll be needing tickets to the games so I can cheer you on," she said happily.

"Wow, my first day and I already have a fan."

"Totally!" Tracy gasped.

From his office Blake overheard Blake's entry intro to Tracy. He stepped around his huge desk, past the open door and the dozen rows of filing cabinets. "Good morning, Blake."

"Mornin'," Blake greeted. "I'm here to sign the papers."

"Wearing a bathing suit?" Will's left eyebrow rose.

"How better to be in disguise?" Blake chuckled. "That's what I love about this job; I just dress like I normally do and then I don't stand out."

"I can't say I noticed what he was wearing," Tracy interjected.

"Just the lack of it," Will commented. "All right, come on into my office and have a seat." Blake followed Will into the office and shut the door behind him. He took a moment to observe the many rows of filing cabinets, the plaques on the wall and the huge red chair where he quickly decided to sit.

"You're not wet?"

"Naw." Blake shrugged. "I dried up on my walk down here. The waves in Florida are wicked awesome today and your office is only a few blocks from the beach. This will work out great. Now I can surf before work."

"You an early riser?"

"Yup," Blake informed. "I'm up at six every morning."

"How are you at pulling all nighters?"

"Love 'em," Blake admitted. "I can go a few days without sleeping more than a few hours."

"Bless your youth, Blake." Will chuckled, sitting down, and then reaching for a contract from his first cabinet.

"When can I start?"

Will pressed a few buttons on the speaker phone. "Fred, I need to see you when you get a chance. I want you to meet Blake."

A voice answered, saying, "Be there in a minute."

Pulling a pen from out of a holder with a center clock, Will pushed the contract in front of Blake on the desk. Blake took a moment to read the first few lines, flattened the second page and signed his name on the bottom line.

Holding up the last page, he said, "I'm looking forward to being a part of Cilva Investigations."

A knock sounded; Will immediately responded. "Come in, Fred."

The door opened half way and a man in his late fifties strolled in. Wearing a white shirt, tie and dress pants, he appeared exactly the opposite of the very casually dressed Blake.

"Blake Anderson, I presume?" Fred lifted a hand for Blake to shake. "Fred."

Blake shook it. "Pleasure." "I hear you are my new partner."

Fred suddenly coughed, trying to hide the shock of Blake's youth and his non-business-like appearance. "I am looking forward to teaching you the ropes."

"Blake has almost four years experience under his belt already from Blackwell," Will interjected. "This should be easy training for you."

Fred struggled to turn his frown around. "We're on a new case." He turned his attention back to Will. "Did he sign the confidentiality agreement?"

Will held up the contract. "He did."

Fred then added, "We're keeping surveillance on a young woman named Catherine Walters who's in an abusive relationship with a pilot. We're currently gathering information on exactly what her situation is."

"Who hired us—a family member of hers?" Blake wondered.

Fred glanced over to Will. "Should I tell him about Janet?"

Will shook his head no. "Let's keep that information closed."

"You can trust me," Blake promised.

Fred agreed. "Let's see how things go. Janet is something only a few of us need to know."

Blake became intrigued. He leaned over, grinning from ear to ear. "Oh, now I've got to meet this chick."

"In time," Will said, "you'll learn."

Blake wrapped his fingers around to make a big O. "Okay, but you'll see my lips are sealed."

"Go up front and Tracy will give you insurance papers and our benefit program information booklet," Will instructed.

The second Blake walked out and shut the door; Fred questioned Will. "You're kidding, right?"

"I promised my cousin I'd take care of him."

Fred sighed and said, "Blackwell owes us big."

CHAPTER 8

Carrying a suitcase, Dr. Jay Newport stood at the edge of the runway as the sun reflected off his silver sunglasses. He patted down his bright, tropical style shirt searching for his car keys to lock his rented black convertible sports car.

"Ready for some Margaritas?" asked a voice from behind. "They claim to have several different flavors on board."

Jay pivoted to find a familiar large, round dimple-faced friend with a bursting smile. "Will!"

"You Tourist!" Will responded, dropping his bag on the ground. "A hibiscus shirt with… what's this, a pineapple?"

"A disguise. Like the shades?"

"Well, it's different from the ties and long pants you usually wear, but I really don't think this is… the new you, Jay. How's my outfit?" Cilva turned slowly to show off his white jacket and tight blue undershirt. "This is the South Beach style the ladies go for."

"Is that so?"

"Never fails." Will's eyes moved suddenly to the right as a man approached them. "That's him, Lucky Garvis."

"You sure?" the doctor asked.

"Yes," Will verified. "I had a friend at the Department of Motor Vehicles pull up his driver's license photo." Lucky sauntered across the runway toward them, exuding confidence in every step; his shaven face showed no emotion. His eyes were hidden behind small round glasses; his slicked back hair glistened.

"Which one of you is Dr. Neighbors?"

"That would be me," Jay lied. The pilot glanced over the doctor's wildly colored shirt.

"Ignore his bad taste," Will cut in. "I'm Will Smith... field, engineer," Cilva announced.

"I kind of figured you weren't Will Smith, seeing as you're white." Lucky motioned for help to assist with the luggage and glanced at them both before sauntering over. Lucky moved away and then glanced at a luggage handler by the airplane for a moment before coming over.

Will leaned over to the Doctor. "You've got to watch the funny ones. It's been my experience that behind every joke is a bit of truth."

"You *are* Caucasian," the Doctor chuckled, "and Smithfield. You couldn't come up with a better name than Smithfield?"

"At least I didn't use my real profession. We are supposed to be undercover, and you still wanted me to register the flight under a doctor's name?"

"This shirt and these shoes are disguise enough." Jay quieted as the luggage was being loaded onto the plane. "I'm wearing flip flops. Successful doctors don't wear flip flops and I've got two offices. It's the perfect cover."

"Who made up the flip flop rule?"

"I did." Jay headed for the plane. "What kind of scam is this? The luggage handler didn't even acknowledge us. Can you believe I'm paying $3,000 for this treatment?" As they climbed into the jet, the pilot's head popped out right before the doctor entered.

"My name's Lucky Garvis and I'll be your pilot for this flight." He moved back as the two of them boarded.

"I know who you are," the doctor whispered, not wanting the pilot to know that he was the object of their study.

"Good looking fellow," Will muttered.

"For a Jackass!" Jay added quietly. Upon entering the enormous jet, the men noted the giant leather chairs, plasma television, full bar, as well as a poker table at the left. Jay's eyes widened as he sat in one of the two full size recliners; Cilva trailed after him and seated himself beside.

"This is some plane," Will commented. "I haven't been on a private jet with you since that engineering convention with Martina Catrell a few years back. Even that one didn't have leather seats."

Just then Lucky entered the cabin from the cockpit and intoned, "Welcome to Busi-Jet. Our jet service offers top quality flight for the elite, upper class businessman. Most of our clients rent jets for quick private flights. Others hire our planes for convenient business meetings. The bar is always full. Once we are in the air, our stewardess, Kat, will help you."

"Kat, as in Kitty?" Will smiled.

"Just Kat," replied Lucky.

From behind a curtain appeared a tall, thin, blonde woman with very large breasts. Wearing high heeled shoes and a white stewardess uniform with the words Busi-Jet written in small blue letters below her collar, she exclaimed with enthusiasm, "Yes, Sir!"

"This is Will Smithfield and Dr. Neighbors. They are our passengers for the next hour. Please be sure to take good care of them."

"Of course, Sir. Here at Busi-Jet," she leaned over Will fastening his seatbelt, "we offer full-service flights."

Will tried to keep his eyes higher than her very large bosom which overflowed from a low-cut, tight, white dress. "Looks like I'm flying Busi-Jet from now on if your hostesses keep looking like Kat."

"I'll be back once we're in the air." She hurried behind the curtain while Will's eyes followed her every move.

"Will," called the doctor as he watched Lucky coming into the cabin to lock the door.

"Ummmm," he gulped.

"Will, look." The doctor quietly pointed to the man in front of them. Lucky's jacket bulged in what could very well have been a gun. The doctor sat back. "See it?"

When Lucky grabbed the cockpit's door handle, Will checked out the suspicious bulge by leaning out to get a better look. When Lucky glanced back at him, Will sat back in his seat.

"We'll be in the air in the next few minutes; strap up and once we reach altitude, Kat will come back to serve you drinks," Lucky announced unemotionally.

Will watched the pilot return to the cockpit. After the door shut, Will opened up his own jacket to reveal the magnum tucked inside his belt. "We're fine."

"Just remember why we are here. We're here to help Catherine Walters, my patient," the doctor reminded.

"I don't intend to kill anyone."

"I'm talking about the stewardess," the doctor reminded. "Stay focused."

"Oh yeah, her."

"Try getting some information on what type of guy this pilot is from Kat. I already have some idea of what kind of company this is."

"You know who that handler was that stuffed our luggage onto the plane?" Will questioned.

"Who?"

"Frank Miller. He's the son of a Randy Miller, the Key West Drug Lord. Whatever he's doing with Busi-jet can't be good. It makes me wonder what kind of pull Lucky has in that arena."

"So, you think his father might use these planes," Jay said, adding two and two. "Miller could be transporting drugs outside the States."

"If the Millers are the kind of thugs Lucky hangs out with, Catherine's in a hell of a lot more trouble than with an abusive boyfriend."

CHAPTER 9

After the plane reached altitude, beautiful blonde Kat pranced into the cabin. She sat down on the sofa across from Will, slowly crossing her shapely legs. She leaned over to fasten a strap on her high heeled shoes. Will was fixated. His finger shot up to his collar, loosening his shirt, and he was cocking his head as he followed every move of Kat's feminine curves.

"Gentlemen, would you like a drink?" she questioned wispily.

"Margarita," Dr. Newport commented, very amused by Kat's obvious attempts of displaying her sexuality.

"Raspberry, perhaps?" she questioned. The doctor slowly nodded in reply. "And you, Mr. Smithfield?"

"Call me Will," he said. "I'll have a light beer." She rose slowly, then walked back behind the curtain with Will's eyes watching her every move.

"Be back soon." Will excused himself from the seat beside the doctor.

"Going after her?" the doctor questioned.

"To get her phone number," Will responded.

"This is the perfect time to find out what you can about Lucky."

Will hurried behind the curtain after the stewardess. The doctor grabbed the newspaper next to his seat and started to read the weather section. It wasn't long before he heard laughter and guessed Will was probably ignoring his request.

Suddenly, the cockpit door opened and Lucky stepped out. Realizing he wasn't piloting, the doctor quickly asked, "Who's flying the plane?"

Lucky grinned. "Fred Miller; he's your co-pilot. Didn't I introduce you?"

The doctor remembers that he'd seen a young man who had placed the luggage on the plane and the same person Will had mentioned as being the son of one of the Key West drug lords. "Yes, of course."

Lucky opened the cabinet and began thumbing through some paperwork. "It won't be long before we land."

More laughter erupted from behind the curtain. Lucky briefly looked up and then returned his attention back to a chart. The doctor noted his carefree reaction; Lucky didn't seem to be bothered that Will was alone with Kat.

"I hope the stewardess isn't your girlfriend," the doctor commented. "My friend has a way with the ladies."

Lucky shrugged. "Kat isn't a one-man woman."

"Oh, then she's not yours. Are you married, then?" the doctor asked.

"I've been thinking about asking my girlfriend Catherine to marry me for my birthday next month."

"I see."

"Have you tied the knot already, Doctor?" Lucky asked, simply.

"I have someone I'm interested in."

"You'll have to bring her next time," he suggested. "I'm sure she'd love South Beach. It's quite a wonderful place to shop high end retail. Even the Kardashians shop there."

"Is your girlfriend a pilot, too?"

"No, Catherine has never flown. In fact, I once tried to get her to go on a skiing trip with me to Colorado. I got her up two steps on and she vomited."

"Really?"

"Is there a pill for that, Doctor?" Lucky wondered. "If there is I'd sure like to have her on it. You have no idea how embarrassing it is to have a girlfriend who won't fly. When we go traveling, I actually have to rent an RV. It used to really bother me but now I consider it a break from being in the air all the time."

"Maybe she isn't the right woman for you then."

Lucky grinned. "Catherine's the best thing that's ever happened to me."

"A man in love?"

Lucky said, "I'm hopeful she'll say yes."

"You're not sure she'll accept your proposal?" The doctor refolded the newspaper on his lap.

"We've had some recent troubles, but I think they are all behind us now. I couldn't imagine life without her."

Suddenly, Kat rushed from behind the curtain with Will. She handed the doctor a blue drink in a very large margarita glass. Will sat down and picked up the beer off her tray.

"Thanks for your cell number," Will said, appreciatively.

"I'm going to show you the best dance club on South Beach," Kat announced. The doctor watched Kat winking goodbye. She looked already smitten with Will's rugged, bad boy image.

"Aren't you supposed to be flying this thing?" Will asked Lucky, repositioning himself down in the big, leather chair.

"Miller is flying us now," the doctor quickly informed Will.

Will, noticing that Lucky had turned his attention back to them, quickly changed the subject. "Told you. I would get it." Will waved the piece of paper with a phone number.

Lucky interrupted. "Kat will probably take you to The Spin Bottles. She goes every time we land in Miami and winds up the belle of the ball. She has yet to find a dance partner who can keep up."

"She hasn't been out grinding with me," Will said. "Wait until she sees my moves. Trust me."

"You can't dance, Will," the doctor curtly said.

"I can't do fancy waltzes, like you, but I know how to shake my rear." Will pivoted to Lucky. "You hear me, right?"

"I'm sure you two will enjoy yourselves," Lucky glanced at the doctor. "No matter where Kat takes you, South Florida clubs are some of finest in the world."

The doctor added, "My friend will just embarrass himself like he did in Mexico."

Lucky quickly inquired, "What happened in Mexico?"

"Will made a dirty dancing attempt and his pants were too big, and they fell down showing his neon speedos. Two bouncers grabbed Will and warned him if he didn't leave the bar immediately, they were calling the police and having him arrested for indecent exposure."

"I started weightlifting that year and had lost a lot of weight," Will explained.

"At least your pants falling down got you to stop dancing," the doctor said and chuckled.

Lucky grinned. "I might just show up at The Spin Bottles to check out these killer moves."

"Kat should bring you along," the doctor told Lucky.

Lucky chuckled. "I can't turn that offer down," he said and then he headed back inside the cockpit to join Fred Miller.

Will suddenly leaned over and said in the doctor's ear, "Why would Lucky take the time to hang out with two clients he doesn't know? This has got to be one hell of a club."

CHAPTER 10

Blake's attention had been drawn to the large beach house and Catherine who was gathering the mail; he hadn't noticed the giant man approaching when a tap sounded on the window of the automobile. Blake nearly jumped out of the passenger's side of Fred's small sedan. Fred rolled down Blake's window and leaned over to see who had just knocked on their surveillance vehicle. The second he saw the big frame and the scruffy face, he grimaced. "Good morning, Hayden."

"Well, if it isn't our local Private Investigators." The man flashed his detective badge. "And you are?"

"I'm Blake Anderson. And you, dude?"

"Detective Carl Hayden," he announced coldly.

Blake studied the undercover detective for a moment. Hayden's middle- aged face had crow's feet around the eyes. With a giant jaw that could handle any fist, Hayden appeared as rough and tough as a man could get. He wore a black trench coat, chain belt, long hair and was heavily tattooed. Blake gazed back in the side mirror to see if Hayden had arrived in a police car, but his ride was a large black motorcycle parked behind them halfway down the street.

"Nice bike," Blake commented.

"What are you two doing in this neighborhood?" Hayden asked Fred.

"We're just visiting the beach," Fred said, matter-of-factly. "Blake is new to the area, a surfer. He wanted to check out our local swells."

With a roll of his black eyes, Hayden showed his disbelief. "Fred, you wouldn't be staking out anyone in my territory?"

Fred replied firmly, "What we are doing here is not a police concern."

Hayden pushed back his trench coat to reveal that he was carrying a gun strapped to his belt. "Just as long as I don't get any complaints about two vagrants looking suspicious."

"We're here to serve our clients."

Hayden moves closer to Blake. "And what about him?"

"Blake's a new employee. Will hired him to replace Ken Minors."

"Sorry to hear about Kenny," Hayden replied quietly. "I was surprised when I heard."

"He couldn't handle the messes we get ourselves in," Fred explained. "He's working for the Parole Board now."

"Good for him," Hayden tagged.

Fred added, "Last I heard, he's doing well and likes the job a lot more than being a PI."

Hayden chuckled from deep in his throat. "Will's not the easiest boss?"

"Will is just fine," Fred said. "Now if you don't mind, we should be getting back to the beach."

"You better watch out," Hayden warned Blake. "Kenny couldn't handle the job after two months, kid."

"I'm twenty-two and old enough to kick your sorry ass," Blake commented. "Stop calling me kid."

Hayden chuckled low, then clutched his side in roaring laughter until he had to lean on the car. "You have no idea who you are dealing with."

"Shut up," Blake said.

Immediately Fred warned Blake, "Watch your mouth, Blake. He's still an undercover cop."

"You think I can't take this overgrown chump!" Blake made a fist. "Right here, right now!"

Hayden patted Blake on the shoulder. "Calm down, kid. I didn't come over to fight Will's latest Magnum wanna be."

"Oh, that's so it, dude." Blake grabbed the car handle to exit the vehicle. Immediately, Hayden blocked the door with his leg; the door didn't budge. "Like I said, it's not a day for beating up the youth. I've got a lot of paperwork on my desk and messing up a baby face isn't on my priority list."

Blake stopped trying to get out of the sedan and plopped back down, glaring at Fred. "You let him talk to us like that?"

"Fred doesn't have a choice after all his parking tickets," Hayden took a step back, reminding him. "One more and he'll lose his license."

"The cops up north lay off and don't act like creeps, man," Blake interjected.

"Then move back, kid." Hayden walked away, grabbed his motorcycle and rode off with his braided hair flying.

Fred apologized. "Sorry about that, Blake. Most of the cops around here are super cool. Hayden doesn't get along with Will. It's a long story but Will used to be on the force until he realized cops have to follow protocol."

A limousine pulled around the corner down the street. They both quieted as the long, black car rolled slowly into the driveway of the two-story beachside home. Slowly the garage door rose, then closed as the limo entered, blocking their view of it and who was arriving. "Damn it!" Fred's hands hit the steering wheel.

Just then the garage door rolled back up and the shiny vehicle backed out of the driveway and headed toward the highway. "Shouldn't we follow the limousine?" Blake asked Fred.

"I don't know. Catherine could still be inside," Fred reminded. "We should stay put. From what I know, Catherine usually doesn't go anywhere without Lucky. Currently, he's flying Will to South Beach."

"Now that's where I'd like to be right now." Blake gave a blissful smile. "I love the North Shore waves. They're ripping."

"It's not a pleasure trip. Will is taking a longtime friend there as part of this assignment to cover Lucky, Catherine's boyfriend."

"That's the pilot, right?"

"Yes," Fred verified. "Will is trying to uncover just how dangerous Lucky truly is."

Blake's attention returned to the beachside home. "I got this bad feeling our girl Catherine is in the limousine and we just lost her."

CHAPTER 11

A bright red neon sign blinked *The Spin Bottles Club* as the doctor and Will approached the enormous white brick building in their rented black convertible. Jay handed the keys over to a valet, noticing the long line outside the club. Every time one of the six bouncers opened the door to let another in, the music thumped loudly out the door.

"Now this is something!" Will gasped, straightening his long black jacket. "These girls are hotter than this Miami heat!"

The doctor tipped the valet with a twenty-dollar bill and headed toward the line. It wasn't long before Kat appeared at the door and waved them forward. They paced past the line toward the scantily dressed Kat and toward the intimidating bouncers.

Will couldn't take his eyes off what Kat was wearing. He followed her long legs to what appeared to be a hot pink bikini and black skirt melded together by an array of long leather straps. "You look amazing!" he announced, taking her arm.

"Thanks. I saved us a table." Kat glanced over to the doctor and winked. He didn't wink back but followed them as two guards opened the door.

When he entered, he studied his surroundings. The giant building had only two levels with a long high ceiling. The center of the first floor was the dance floor, a giant, slow-moving turntable of glass. Lights glowed beneath it, illuminating the imported beer bottle collection underneath. Most of the crowded dancers were bumping and grinding against one another to hot Latin music.

Kat, Will, and the doctor snaked through the dancers to the left side where dozens of tables were set up near the packed bar. Those who were admitted into this area knew how to dress.

After they had passed two tables near the dancers, the doctor spotted their pilot Lucky. Next to him was a young woman he guessed to be in her early twenties. She had spiked, bright red hair and a small nose ring.

"Lucky," the doctor greeted, sitting down.

"This is Abby, Doctor Neighbors," the pilot said, introducing the woman. Obviously, this wasn't Catherine, the doctor concluded and wondered if Lucky was already cheating on his patient.

"She is my younger sister and lives here in Miami," Lucky added. The second the doctor sat down, Abby moved over to him and whispered in his ear, "Want to dance."

The doctor admitted, "Maybe later. I'm thirsty."

"What can I get for you?" she inquired, gulping down a red drink. "Bloody Mary, like me?"

"Margarita." He smiled, displaying perfectly white teeth.

"I'll be right back." Abby stood, revealing a skirt that barely covered her derriere. Then she turned on a five inch heel, heading toward the bar.

"She's a little hungry tonight," Lucky told the doctor. "I should have warned you about my sister."

"She's lovely, I'm sure," the doctor said and grinned.

Will and Kat returned with several imported bottles of beer. Kat popped open a bottle, gulped it till it was gone, and then asked Will, "Are you ready to show off those famous moves?"

"You don't want to see them," the doctor reminded her.

"Yes, I do." Kat grabbed Will's hand and pulled him up.

The second the next song started, a pop song with a prominent bass line, they edged onto the dance floor. Will did a quick turn and Kat yelped with joy. Together, they molded, with Will's arms flailing about like an injured bird. It was all the doctor could do not to chuckle.

"Here you go, Doc." Abby returned and handed him his Margarita. As she sat down, he couldn't help noticing that she wasn't wearing anything underneath but a very small thong. His hand encircled a frosted margarita glass—strawberry—not his favorite flavor but it would do, he decided.

His lips sucked down some of the icy drink and then he took in the dancers, trying hard not to stare at Abby. She was so blatantly obvious about her interest in him.

"So, what kind of doctor are you?" she asked.

"Shrink," he said, matter-of-factly.

"Good. I may have issues, Doc," she replied as her hand dropped to rub his knee.

Ignoring the strokes, the doctor continued to drink. "I thought you wanted to dance."

"I want many things."

"Don't you have any self-esteem?"

Her hand shot away from his leg. "Excuse me."

"I must say, a woman this forward really isn't thinking of impressing a man with her intelligence."

"What?"

"Were you abused or abandoned by a father figure?" he asked. "Are you desperately seeking the attention of other men to fill that need to have a man in your life?"

Her big brilliant green eyes narrowed into a squint. "You're weird."

"So, which was it, abused or abandoned?"

"I'm not in the mood for this." She stood.

He grabbed her hand. "Wait a minute," the doctor said, suddenly listening to the changing song. "This is a rumba."

"Let go of me, freak!"

The doctor pulled Abby onto the dance floor and began to sway to the beat, faster than he was used to. Abby stared at him for several seconds and noticed how he attracted attention with his incredible, precision moves; even Kat and Will took notice.

"Ready?" The doctor shot out his hand for Abby to accept the invitation to dance with him.

She followed his lead, and they melded together across the floor like two hot ravishing bodies. The doctor was in his element. His hips swayed easily with excellent control as his upper body led his partner. He turned so gracefully that he made it look easy.

"You're incredible," Abby shouted.

"My mother owns a dance studio. I worked there through college. And you aren't half bad."

"I love dancing." Abby leaned over and whispered into his ear, "With you."

"I prefer two dances, the rumba and the tango. The tango, I reserve for only special occasions and with a special partner."

The doctor twirled her around and around until he cupped her back and leaned her down as the music ended. Their lips almost touched before he mumbled, "Freak!"

"Yes," she gasped, breathlessly enchanted. "I like the way you dance." Some of the audience nearby applauded their performance. When they stood back up, the doctor felt a hand on his shoulder. Will walked up to him and put his hand on his shoulder.

Will pulled him back. "Check out who's at our table now," he warned.

The doctor checked behind him and found Fred Miller talking to Lucky. Next to him was another man, older, wearing a pair of sunglasses and holding a cane in his left hand. "Who is that?"

"Only the Drug Lord of Key West, Fred Miller's father."

"You're kidding?" the doctor hoped. "Here, in Miami?"

"We just found ourselves in a whole different kind of company." Will was grateful for the feel of a gun under his arm. "Stay close and don't say anything that would reveal who we are."

"Do you really think they'll care I'm a doctor?"

"If they find out I'm a private investigator, there is no way they are going to believe all this was over some patient of yours! So, keep quiet."

Then from the right side of the dancers, Catherine appeared in a short black dress and a red spider web belt. Her hair had been cut shoulder length, but there was no doubt in his mind, it was his Catherine. The doctor couldn't believe he was busted. How could he explain this? How could he tell her he was checking out her boyfriend without looking like a stalker?

Will guessed, "By the way you're staring at that hot brunette who just sat down. I'm guessing she's your patient, Catherine Walters."

"Now what?" The doctor looked a little frantic.

"Follow my lead." Will headed toward the drug lord's roundtable.

CHAPTER 12

With her eyes widening with recognition, Catherine gasped and said, "Doctor Newport, you look so different without a tie."

The doctor glanced down at his tropical shirt. "I'm vacationing in Miami with a friend of mine. This is Will, Catherine," he said, introducing him.

"I didn't know you were dating my boyfriend's sister, Abby," Catherine said, surprisingly.

"We just met," Abby quickly explained, taking the seat next to Catherine. "And I thought his last name was Neighbors."

"Conflict of interest," the doctor said.

"Conflict of interest?" Lucky snarled. "Sit down, Doc. You aren't screwing my sister or my girlfriend."

Abby gazed at the doctor longingly. "If I had things my way, we already would have."

"Will and I must be leaving," the doctor announced.

"We have an early appointment in the morning to discuss some building plans of mine," Will explained.

"You can't leave yet, Will," Kat protested. "We just started dancing and you haven't even finished your drink."

"Next trip," Will promised.

Lucky stood. "You two find out you know Catherine and all of a sudden you need to take off."

"He's my doctor," Catherine explained.

"What kind of doctor?" Lucky asked.

"A shrink," Abby announced.

"Psychiatrist?" Lucky grabbed Catherine's arm fast and forcefully. "What is all this about? What have you been telling him?"

"Nothing about us." Catherine winced in pain.

Will leaned forward and plucked Lucky's hand off of Catherine's forearm. "Lay off the lady."

"This is none of your business!" Lucky snapped, and then turned to Catherine. "Now what the hell are you complaining about? I give you everything! Everything! You don't want for anything!"

"I am not a relationship therapist," the doctor interjected.

Catherine quickly agreed, seeing that Lucky began to back away. "Yes, I'm seeing him about my mom. I told you she just got diagnosed with breast cancer. Remember? I'm having a hard time dealing with the possibility of losing her."

Jay didn't know her mom had cancer. He wondered if Catherine's story was a cover up. If it were true, she might need further counseling help dealing with a family illness. Regardless, with the news Lucky no longer seemed angry. Quietly, he sat down and drank the rest of his beer, then smiled at the doctor.

"I didn't think you'd mind. That's why I didn't mention it," Catherine added.

"Your mother is about to have an operation and start chemo treatments," Lucky remembered, coldly.

"I knew you would understand why I would need some anxiety medication." Catherine gave him a kiss on the cheek.

By now, Doctor Newport had a hand on his stomach, wincing at a stab of pain. In less than five minutes, Lucky had showed his true nature. Controlling and violent, he was exactly the way Catherine had described Lucky. Jay wondered if she even knew that there were drug dealers at this table, dangerous ones.

"Do you really have to leave so soon Doctor?" Catherine entreated. "It's wonderful seeing you outside the office."

"It's best we keep a professional relationship."

Abby begged, saying, "Dancing with you was like a dream. Please stay a while longer. You should see him, Catherine! Your doctor has incredible moves."

Catherine retorted, "Yes, he seemed to really enjoy dancing with you, Abby."

Suddenly a smile appeared on the doctor's face. He liked hearing the hint of jealousy in Catherine's voice. He had thought she was attracted to him, but that slight anger in her voice was proof. She was trying to hide it, but she certainly couldn't hide the way she gazed at him.

"There's no reason to go, Doctor Newport. Please enjoy yourself. This is Frank Miller; he's a local real estate developer. It seems you've already gotten to know my boyfriend, Lucky," Catherine continued.

"I flew them here to Miami," Lucky announced.

"Amazing!" Catherine said. "Out of all the planes in the world you wound up renting my boyfriend's."

Will winked. "We really should be going. I have an early meeting. It's nice to meet you, Catherine."

"See you tomorrow night for the flight back, Doctor Neighbors." Lucky then corrected himself. "Uh, Newport."

"I can explain the name change."

"Don't bother, Doctor. It happens often in my business. Men with wives getting away for the weekend." Lucky grinned.

Will nudged the doctor's arm and inched him away from the table, heading for the door. Will glanced back and when he was sure no one was following them, he hurried the doctor outside. The valet came with the black sports car before the doctor even pulled out his ticket. He grabbed another twenty from his wallet and handed it to the valet.

"Thanks," the valet said and waved in response. Doctor Newport got behind the wheel and Will immediately jumped in on the passenger's side.

Will said, "That was one hell of a way to blow a cover, Jay."

"I thought we handled it well," the doctor said, sarcastically.

"By now every drug dealer in Key West knows who we are," Will reminded. "This isn't really undercover anymore."

"I know."

Will added, "Your patient's boyfriend pilots a bunch of private jet planes for drug dealers. Good luck with that." There was silence for a moment as the doctor sped the car through traffic and headed down toward the long drive by the beach. He took a few deep breaths and then stopped the car on the boardwalk.

"What did you think of her?" the doctor asked.

"Of Catherine Walters?" Will questioned.

"Isn't she different?"

"A Greek Goddess. I wasn't expecting to find your latest to be so hot." Will pulled out his cell phone and dialed a number. The conversation started quickly.

The doctor couldn't hear what was going on other than, "Yes, sure… okay… so that's why… okay."

Will folded up the cell phone. "Fred said they lost Catherine about four hours ago. He and Blake were parked around the corner when a limousine pulled into the garage. He couldn't see who got in the limousine, so he wasn't sure if he should follow the car."

"We should have more eyes on this," the doctor announced.

"I got a bad feeling on this one," Will advised. "I think it is best we leave Catherine and her boyfriend's drug lord cohorts alone."

The doctor shook his head no. "Not a chance."

"Trust me. Let this one go, Jay. Catherine's trouble with a capital T."

"There's something about her," the doctor ruminated. "She's got potential."

Cilva pulled out a cigar and a lighter. He lit one and began to smoke, watching a large wave crash onto the shore. Two couples passed the car walking out onto the white sandy beach carrying blankets. "You've got to learn. You can't save the world."

"Just an abused woman or two." Jay grinned.

"Can't talk you out of this one?" Will questioned.

"Not with Catherine."

"You like her." Will figured it out.

"She reminds me of someone."

"Yeah, and I know who. That's what worries me." Will puffed on his cigar.

"Don't worry. I can handle it."

"Then you give me no alternative, Jay, but to stick my neck out on tomorrow's flight I'll need to find out more about Lucky and hope I won't get my throat slit in the process."

CHAPTER 13

The presidential suite Lucky had rented was exquisite. Large rooms were filled with fine furniture as well as small touches like hand carved sea turtles. All the amenities were being included such as a welcome basket of fruit and champagne, seventy-two-inch plasma television which hung among fine impressionist reproductions of Monet. But for Catherine, it wasn't the gold leafed tables or paintings that impressed her; it was the midnight view of the ocean below.

"I'll put your bags in the bedroom," the bellhop informed her; then he went to the bedroom on the right. "Would you like me to show you how to use the Jacuzzi tub, Miss?"

"No, thank you," Catherine responded.

"The bar is fully stocked and there is a room service menu on the coffee table." Catherine checked her wallet for a tip but realized that Lucky hadn't given her any money. How would she tip?

"Tips have already been taken care of," the motel employee immediately added. "Is there anything else that I can do for you?"

"No, not now. Thank you."

"If you need extra towels just call down to the front desk and we'll be more than happy to bring more." He bowed. "Thank you for staying at the Miami Ocean." Catherine smiled at the employee before he left her alone in the gigantic suite. Most women would be thrilled to stay in such a room. In fact, she knew most had never had such a privilege. Lucky did provide all the joys money could bring. She wondered if she'd miss these things.

Slowly, she stepped out onto the balcony. The water was so black in the distance, where the water ended and the dark sky met could not be determined. Below the waves rolled in with white caps, slapping at the shore. The smell of salt stung her nose and she took in another deep breath, loving the sea. The door behind her opened. No longer alone, she turned to find Lucky standing behind her.

She greeted, saying, "Our room is lovely."

"Only the best for you." He closed the gap between them.

She couldn't help noticing his lowered voice. Normally, she'd take this as a warning to leave the room. Sometimes time and space diffused volatile situations with Lucky, but this time she wanted to know what was troubling him. She believed it had to do with what happened at the club.

"I don't want you to be Newport's patient anymore," Lucky announced. How many times he'd spoken against her previous physicians and picked new ones for her, she remembered, but now she must ignore his request.

"There is nothing wrong with Dr. Newport. He is a fine doctor and I find him easy to talk to."

"That's the problem." Lucky put his hands on her shoulders. "I don't like you opening up to strangers."

"A friend of my mother's suggested his office and since my stress has to do a lot with my mother and how she is feeling, I think he's appropriate. Besides, if I don't go to him, I'll go to another."

"There's nothing wrong with your mind," Lucky pressed. "And your mother can handle her own problems."

Catherine tried to back away, but his hands tightened their grip, stopping her from moving away. "My sister now… she's a real wacko," Lucky interjected. "After the doctor left, she drank half a bottle of vodka, babbling how she blew things with the best dancer she had ever met. She doesn't even know Newport and neither do you. I don't like your telling our business to a complete nobody."

"He's gifted," Catherine confessed. "I need help dealing with all this anxiety."

Lucky released his grip, shaking his head with frustration. "I don't think a shrink is necessary."

"I need medication!"

"I don't want my life known!" Lucky shouted.

Catherine started to get the feeling that he was concerned about more than not wanting another man's perspective on their troubled relationship. "That's easy enough to solve. I won't mention you. I'll just talk about my anxiety and the medication. Would that make you feel better?"

"I don't trust him or Will with any information about us, especially my business."

She took a few strides and stood on the edge of the balcony. For a moment, she turned her thoughts away from him to the ocean below. In the distance, she could see a ship, with one single light guiding its way across the sea. It was a big ship, perhaps a cruise liner or a commercial fishing vessel.

"Catherine? Hello? Are you even paying attention?" Lucky asked, rudely.

She turned to face him, hiding her tiredness of being so controlled. "I'm sorry, but I will continue to have Doctor Newport as my doctor whether you like it or not."

Will's anger was apparent. His face reddened and his teeth clenched; his words spewed out like daggers. "When you're finished," he said, grabbing the balcony door and moving inside, "come to bed. I have to set the alarm early so I won't miss flying those two idiots back."

Catherine hated the insult but chose not to speak. She whirled around to stare at the waves once more. The door slammed behind her, and she heard his feet tread heavily toward the bedroom.

Another night, sleeping next to him. How could she face another night lying next to that man? Did he even care for her at all? Why shouldn't he want her to have a good doctor? Why all these secrets about his business?

Her mind drifted back to Doctor Newport dancing with Abby in the club and Will with his arms wrapped around Kat. Two attractive men: gorgeous, smart and sexy. She couldn't help but feel a little jealous of Kat and Abby. Neither of them would harm her in the ways Lucky had, or at least that's the way they seemed. Doctor Newport and Will were so different than Lucky or her father.

"Catherine!" Lucky roared. "Get in here!"

CHAPTER 14

Catherine shivered. The very thought of Lucky's arms around her as she slept made her shiver. The past week spending time with her mother, swimming, enjoying their time without Lucky, felt like a lifetime away.

"Catherine!"

How long could she pretend not to hear his calling? A part of her wished she could sleep on the patio underneath the stars. As her eyes drifted up, she realized how big a galaxy this was. Surely, there was room for both of them, enough space for them to live apart.

"Catherine!"

So many times he called her name. It was an order… not much different than calling a dog, she supposed. Lucky cared for her, took care of her basic needs, but she only got treats if she obeyed his every whim. Sit. Stand. Come.

What kind of dog had she become?

Was she a poodle: smart, yet careful about appearance? *No*, she thought, *I'm all or none. Poodles are beautiful with great spirit; they are beautiful and divine in spirit.* Perhaps, she was more like a bassett hound: lazy, cute and slow. Then again, maybe she'd just be turning into a German shepherd: intelligent and guarded.

"Catherine!" His voice sharpened.

She better go before she risked the consequences of reprimand. Dogs do get punished by masters when they don't do as they are told. Maybe she should go into the bedroom and pee on the floor.

That would be funny but not practical. Surely, the motel would charge a cleaning fee. Catherine took one last look at the ocean and wished she were on that boat so far away. The light seemed to be calling her onto the sea. On the ship, isolated in God's magnificent creation. What bliss!

She opened the door and slowly walked to the bedroom. Lucky was unclothed and lying in bed with the blanket to his waist. He was an attractive man: tan, thin and tall. She had once been drawn to him like a moth to a flame.

"Come." He rolled down the blanket.

In his nakedness, her confusion grew. Her revulsion was mixed with sexual need. Her eyes closed as she undressed and got underneath the covers. She pictured Will holding Kat.

Men aren't going for overweight and crazy, she reminded herself. She was right where she belonged, wasn't she? As Lucky leaned over and gently kissed her lips, she felt his hands over her body.

Immediately, she pushed his hand away from her breast. "I am tired," she said, coldly.

"That was quite a drive for you," Lucky murmured against her lips. "You could always take the jet back."

"You know I hate to fly." Catherine gulped. "Please don't make me."

Lucky kissed her again. "Don't worry. The company limousine will be downstairs in the morning."

Catherine breathed a sigh of relief against his lips. "Thank you."

"I love you," he said.

"I hate when we argue," Catherine admitted.

"You really want to keep Doctor Newport?" he asked, staring directly into her grayish-blue eyes.

"I think he's an excellent physician." Catherine didn't move her gaze into his eyes. She wanted him to believe her.

"That's all there is to it, right? This isn't about us."

"Why are you having doubts?" Catherine smiled at him.

Lucky tossed a hand through his hair and glanced back down. "You're right. I have no idea why this bothers me so much. Your main concern has been your mother lately."

"Of course, it has!" Catherine raised her voice and then leaned back. "My mother only has me since my father left and she needs me right now more than ever. Her recovery from breast cancer is my highest priority."

"Even over me?" Lucky sighed.

"Can't you understand that?" Catherine asked him.

Suddenly his eyes closed and then for a minute he stared up at the tall ceiling, contemplating. Then in one rush movement, he scooped her body up in his hands and began to caress her frame.

"Lucky, I really am not feeling well."

He didn't detour from his attempts at distracting her with his kisses. Over and again, he put his lips against her skin. Although she was tempted to push away his hands, she was drawn deeper.

She should scream for him not to ever touch her again. Yet, Lucky knew the way she liked to be loved. He rose and pulled apart her legs. His large warm frame pushed against hers.

"I want you, Catherine," he groaned.

His manhood swelled and pressed against her petals. With his hands rubbing her breasts, he moved his lips from her mouth to her right nipple. He licked at it with his tongue, making her wet with desire.

"We shouldn't," Catherine whispered.

"Forget our fight," Lucky moaned.

Catherine tried to ignore every cry of her body to allow him to claim her. "I can't. I'm angry at you right now. Maybe in the morning we can, after I have time to calm down."

He didn't hear her or didn't care. He pushed himself into her, widening her to the brim. She let out a cry, half mad, but the rest of her passionately accepted his manhood. Her hips rose and met his every thrust.

With mixed emotions, her mind chose to ignore rational thinking and answer only to something far more primitive. Raw, pounding flesh, they rubbed their bodies against one another until they both screamed out in climax. Her nails drawing into his back skin, Catherine cried out again, and he collapsed onto his elbows, catching his breath.

He said, once, "I love you, Catherine." Then he rolled over, gave her one last kiss. "I have a meeting in the morning before the flight," he said and then he fell asleep with a loud snort.

CHAPTER 15

At sunrise, Dr. Newport and Will boarded the Busi-jet plane where Kat greeted them with drinks. Will took a beer and quickly kissed her cheek, but the doctor refused his Margarita.

Kat said, "Maybe you'll want a drink once we are in the air."

"Perhaps." Jay sat down next to Will.

The lights flickered in the cabin. "Buckle up, we're about to take off." Kat hurried behind the curtain. A few seconds passed and the plane's engine started. The jet sped down the runway and rose into the azure-blue, cloudless Florida sky.

After a half hour, Lucky opened the cockpit door and entered the plane's cabin. "Almost landing time."

Kat brought Will another beer, but the doctor refused the red margarita, again.

"I think you both should take some advice and don't ever book Busi-Jet again," Lucky curtly said, staring down at the doctor.

The doctor didn't appear surprised. "Why is that?" he responded, noticing Lucky's right-hand knuckles were raw as if he had punched someone. "I find Busi-Jet planes perfect for short trips."

"We don't fly private investigators." Lucky turned his glare to Will.

"He's a P.I.?" Kat gasped. "Neat! I've always wanted to date one of those Magnum types."

Lucky suddenly raised his voice. "Kat, make me a pot of coffee and strap in for landing!"

Will watched Kat dart behind the curtain; then he turned his eyes to Lucky. His hand slowly lowered to his jacket, and he kept his fingers right above the gun. Will simply state, "Gathering information about my agency didn't take you long."

"Fly Busi-Jet again and you'll both learn exactly who you are dealing with," Lucky snarled as he headed back into the cockpit.

After the plane landed, Kat came out from behind the curtain and opened the side door for them to exit. "Don't forget to call me, Will," she said to Will, then gently kissed him goodbye on the lips.

Outside sat the doctor's parked convertible; Will and Jay made their way down the steps toward their vehicle.

The second Will's passenger side door was shut, Jay exhaled. "How'd Lucky find out your identity so fast?"

"I don't know but that's the least of our worries. Since they know who I am, they have to be wondering just what things Catherine is telling you."

"She doesn't know what kind of business the Millers are in."

"How can you be so sure?" Will questioned.

"Because we wouldn't be alive now," the doctor said confidently. "They would have already assumed she told me they were involved in drugs. Right now, Lucky believes Catherine's cancer story about her mother."

"Which by the way, I wish she would have brought it up before," Will said. "From the information I've gathered so far, her mother is Catherine's only living relative. She'll be out on the street if things don't work out with Lucky. I checked out Catherine's last place of employment, too, an elementary school where she was a teacher's aide. I called the principal who told me that Catherine would show up in the classroom with bruises. He could tell she was lying about how she got them. They gave her some lame excuse about why they had to let her go. Her bruises were sometimes so obvious it upset the kids."

Jay hit the steering wheel with his fist. "That's the worst part: learning what you hoped wouldn't be the truth, is. And what we've learned turns out worse than what Catherine even knows!"

"That's true about a lot of things in life."

"I have a feeling Kat doesn't know who the Millers are either. She was too excited about learning you were a private investigator. Think about it; if she had anything to do with Miller's drugs she wouldn't have been," Jay concluded.

"You want me to go back to Miami next weekend and give Kat a call to find out more?" Will inquired.

"That's your decision."

"If you want my opinion, it's probably best you drop Catherine as a patient."

"I can't do that now." Jay sighed.

"You have plenty of other clients."

"Stop trying to talk me out of helping Catherine," the doctor responded.

"You're risking our lives, Jay."

"She's good-hearted and that's how she got in this mess. I can't turn my back on her. I won't… I can't."

"This job ain't gonna come cheap."

"I know that" the doctor said and smirked. "When have your services ever been cheap?"

Will leaned back against the leather seat. He pulled out his gun and examined it. "Is this how far you are willing to go?"

"I hate violence. You know that."

"Better call in the network then," Will said.

"Janet's friends have never let us down before. The first thing Catherine needs is self-esteem through employment."

"One she can show up bruises for," Will reminded. "That's not going to happen anymore."

"I forgot sometimes how all that money goes to your head." Will stuck his gun back underneath his coat. "You always think you're invincible."

"Money can make me invisible and invincible." Will rubbed his forehead. "Not that angle again."

"You had to know it was coming."

"For the record, I disagree with this new assignment, Jay. There are too many people involved in the network and if word gets out, it's our necks on the line."

"I don't pay you to like your clients," the doctor reminded. "The network will assist Catherine."

"It's not Catherine I'm worried about anymore." Will smirked. "It's us going against the biggest drug lords in Florida's history. That is who Lucky was referring to with that warning he gave us."

Jay returned Will's smirk with an arrogant smile that showed off his perfectly gleaming white teeth. "Someone has to stand up against them."

CHAPTER 16

Catherine jumped out of the limousine before the driver could assist with her door. Outside a one-bedroom townhouse, her mother kneeled in the garden, pulling weeds from around a palm tree, crown-of-thorns, pansy and bird-of-paradise landscaping.

Catherine leaned down and hugged her mom, nearly knocking off her mother's big straw hat. "I just got back from Miami and wanted to stop by." Pleased to see her, her mother smiled. "How are you feeling, Mom?"

"I'm doing a bit better," her mother admitted. "I've been busy keeping my mind off the operation. I went to the movies with my friend Patricia and then to bingo last night. This morning at the garden center, I picked up these pansies to add some brightness to the front yard."

"I love the purple and yellow ones."

"They look happy, don't they?" her mother said. "There's something about pansies that just make one smile."

Catherine waited until her mother rose from her knees, and then gathered her garden tools for her. "You don't have to quit on my account, Mom."

"It's nearly noon."

Looking at the cloudy sky, Catherine added, "But it's not hot and I can help you pull weeds."

"I did buy a few more pallets of flowers." Her mother pointed to the garage. "I put them on the right side of the boxes by the car."

"Good, I'll get them." Catherine walked around the limousine and as soon as the window lowered, she informed the driver, "I won't be needing you further. My mother will give me a ride home once we are done in the garden. Thank you for your services."

The driver tapped his cap. "Have a good day."

"You, too." Catherine strolled back around the limousine and headed toward the garage as the car pulled away.

"What about your dress?" Her mother pointed her trowel at Catherine's designer yellow sundress and matching shoes.

Catherine laughed. "I always dress up for the garden. Don't you remember when I was a little girl and wore my Sunday best to make mud pies?"

Tears came to her mother's eyes; then she nodded. "You're right. At least I stopped you from eating them."

Quickly, Catherine entered the garage and picked up another pallet of pansies with both hands. She noticed that there were two pots of pink crape Myrtles which would grow into trees in a few years.

"Crape Myrtles, too?" Catherine questioned. "They have gorgeous little blooms. Don't they?"

"I bought them with the hope that someday I will see them grow taller than you," her mother said. "I got them in pink so I would think of them like watching you grow up into the stunning woman you've become."

Catherine put down the pallet near the other pansies. She noticed that there was an entire square open in the back of the palm tree and in desperate need of filling with flowers. "You see me through a Mother's eyes."

"Yes," she said. "Lucky doesn't deserve you."

"We had an interesting time in Miami," Catherine informed, kneeling down beside the flowers and grabbing a nearby shovel. "We ran into Abby and Kat. You'll never guess who they were dancing with."

"Kat, the stewardess? I thought you didn't care for her too much."

Catherine sighed. "She's all wrong for Doctor Newport's friend Will."

"Doctor Newport?" her mother questioned. "You ran into him in Miami?"

"Yes," Catherine admitted. "He and his friend Will were vacationing and tried Busi-Jet."

"So, Lucky met your doctor? I wish I'd been a fly on that wall!"

"Lucky doesn't want me to see Doctor Newport anymore," Catherine informed her. "He thinks there is nothing wrong with me."

"From his point-of-view there isn't," her mother reminded her. "He gets whatever he wants and if he doesn't get what he wants, he threatens, insults or tosses you around until you change your mind."

"You're exaggerating."

Her mother approached and knelt to assist in the plantings. "No, I'm concerned."

"Don't be." Catherine suddenly smiled. "I got through to Lucky last night. He will allow me to continue to see Doctor Newport professionally. I just have to behave and not tell the doctor the things Lucky doesn't want him to know."

"Allow?"

"That's not what I meant to say," Catherine corrected. "I didn't mean to say that Lucky will allow me." Her mother slipped a small pansy with a purple and yellow face downward into a hole she had created. Catherine leaned over and placed the dirt around the center to ensure the roots were covered.

"You will continue to talk to the doctor about leaving Lucky, right?"

"Lucky just made it very clear he doesn't want any Busi-Jet information to get leaked. You know Lucky has many rich and famous clients who use his service knowing that their identities and locations must be kept confidential," Catherine added. "Besides, Lucky and I may stay together if he changes his ways."

Her mother's eyes went down to the flower bed. "You know, Darling, raising children and growing plants are very different from one another. A plant needs only three things: good dirt, water and sunshine. A baby needs a lot more. She needs to be nurtured. That means more than just food, water and sunshine. It means love. What you and Lucky have now is choking out your roots. You need space to grow so that your face…" She held up the pansy's face. "…has a way of looking happy again."

Catherine didn't know what to say to that. She just reached down and continued to plant pansies. It didn't take long for hours to pass, both of them enjoying being out underneath the Florida sun and puffy clouds which beckoned an afternoon shower.

CHAPTER 17

"It's going to rain," Blake commented to Fred.

Fred lowered his binoculars to stop watching Catherine and her mother planting flowers in the front yard. "Maybe we should park the sedan closer instead of around the corner."

"This spot's good." Blake grunted. "Catherine might remember this car from when we were beachside."

"Yeah, I suppose we can't risk it."

"I could take my board out of the backseat and skate pass if you want."

"Does that mean you're bored and want to skateboard for a while?" Fred asked, knowingly.

"You got me, dude."

"I know you have that competition coming up but for right now we need to stay focused."

"I hear you." Blake understood. "It's just the waves sucked this morning and I need to get some exercise."

"Surf tomorrow then."

"I got to keep in shape for the games," Blake reminded. "We've been sitting in this car forever."

"For four hours," Fred checked his watch, "and thirty-two minutes."

"I got to piss."

"Walk to the convenience store down the next block over by the highway," Fred said. "It looks like we're going to be here for a while by all those flowers they've still got to plant."

"I can go?" Blake questioned.

"Sure, bring me a soda and a sandwich," Fred ordered. "In fact, a candy bar too. That would be great."

Blake glanced over at him. "You just want the food. Don't you?"

"One of us needs to get grub. You, first. Then after we eat, I'll go to piss. Just call me on this," Fred handed him a walkie-talkie, "if you see or hear anything suspicious."

Blake clipped the tool onto his belt. "This thing's awesome."

"It has a four-block radius. Our company uses them all the time."

"That's great," Blake said. "Then one person could get in closer and listen in to what's going on."

"I don't think so." Fred shrugged. "We just prefer these over cell phones because they can't be traced."

"Cool, dude." Blake opened the car door and exited. "What kind of sandwich you want?"

Fred pulled out a wallet from his back pocket and opened it up. "I got a twenty. Buy what you can with that. When we get back to the office, I'll have Cilva issue you a company credit card."

"I get a card?" Blake's eyes widened with glee.

"Don't get your panties in a bunch." Fred smiled. "Cilva gets the bill, and he goes through everything with a fine-tooth comb. Whatever gets charged better be approved. Food on surveillance usually is but it has to be near the area issued."

"Got it." Blake took the cash.

"Hurry back," Fred reminded him.

From the backseat, Blake grabbed his skateboard. Tossing it to the ground, he planted one foot and skated off quickly. It didn't take him long to get to the store not far from where the car was parked.

When he approached the building, he noticed the motorcycle parked out front and immediately thought twice about entering. Undercover Police Detective Carl Hayden was inside the store.

He found that too much of a coincidence. They had run into this police officer twice in two days. Either it was intentional, or it was just bad luck. Either way Blake paused, wondering if he should go any further.

Hayden left the store, popping open a soda can. He drained the drink in a few big gulps before he saw Blake picking up his skateboard.

Blake greeted him. "Small town, I guess."

"Not so small, kid." Hayden zipped up his jacket.

"Looks like rain. You should be careful on your hog."

"Thanks for the advice." Hayden picked up his helmet off the motorcycle seat and jumped on. "I've been riding longer than you've been alive, kid."

Blake tossed his board over one shoulder and started to walk away. Deciding it would be better not to argue with an undercover police officer three times his size, this time, he headed toward the store's door.

Before putting on his helmet and starting the engine of his bike, Hayden asked, "So what are you doing on this side of town?"

"You own this side too?"

"Not today." Hayden chuckled, deep and long. "Fred around too or are they putting you on your own already?"

"What makes you think I'm working?"

"Looked your new address up, Blake Anderson. You're a far cry away from your apartment with your girlfriend and without a vehicle you're probably here to piss during a long stake out."

"Wrong." Blake whirled around and approached the detective. "I also have to get Fred a sandwich."

"Thought he had a sweet tooth." Hayden's smile dropped. "At least that's what Ken told me after he quit. Fred always has tons of candy bars on long stakeouts."

"Tell me," Blake cocked his head, "why are you so interested in Cilva and his employees?"

Hayden put on his helmet and lifted the shield. "Will Cilva doesn't think twice about breaking the law to get his man. That's why I got him kicked off the force. I got tired of watching him break into houses to gather information. We're supposed to be the good guys not the criminals."

"I don't know anything about that."

"Would you break into houses to get a man behind bars?" Hayden studied Blake. "Problem I have is too many on the force look at Cilva as some kind of vigilante ex-cop. Then there's the doctor and the whole Janet thing. None of that sits well with me, kid. Unlike your crew, I follow the letter of the law even though I'm undercover."

"Like I said. I don't know anything about that. I'm new, remember. Haven't even met Janet."

In a big howl of laughter, Hayden muttered, "If you ever meet Janet then you're in a whole hell of a lot of trouble I can't help you out of, kid." With that, he sped off onto the highway.

CHAPTER 18

Dr. Newport grabbed the file off the secretary's front desk and immediately noticed Catherine through the glass, seated in the packed waiting room. She appeared somewhat nervous, fumbling through the men's magazines on the side table next to her chair. Slight social anxiety, he predicted. He watched her for a minute. She shuffled her feet, uncomfortable in a room full of strangers. Then she sat back, opened a rag trade and began to read.

His secretary hung up the phone. "So, is she the reason you keep coming to my desk this morning?"

He shot back with a grin, took the top file from off the pile and opened the side door. "Catherine, please come in."

Catherine rose, noticing that he was looking at her clothing.

He slowly walked her to his office across the short hallway. "Good to see you again, Catherine."

"Thank you." She sat in the side chair instead of the sofa and sat down across from him.

The doctor opened the folder, seated himself at the desk and began to look through it as she waited patiently to be addressed. "Did you like the prescription?" he asked.

Catherine admitted, "I need refills."

"No side effects then?" he questioned.

"It bothered my tummy a bit, but then I started taking it with food and noticed that it helped."

"Food with that medicine is fine." He couldn't help but stare at her. She was really trying hard to fight her attraction. She wouldn't quite look him in the eye, but when she did, there was a hint of guilt.

"It was wonderful running into you in Miami. Are you going to continue to date Lucky's sister, Abby?"

"She's not my type," he admitted honestly.

"I didn't think so." Catherine grinned. "Quite frankly she goes through so many men, every time I meet Lucky in Miami, she has another boyfriend or two. Really, you'd be wasting your time dating her."

"I see."

"She's not a very genuine person either. I've caught her snickering behind my back and making fun of my weight."

"Like I said, Abby is not my type," the doctor repeated.

"I'm glad."

"I find it fascinating that you would take such an interest enough to warn me about someone I just met." The doctor hid his amusement. "Normally my patients stay out of my personal life."

Catherine's smile faded.

"But since you are so forward as to try to determine the quality of the person I should date, let me ask. Who do you think I should be dating?"

"Oh, I'm sorry." Catherine gasped. "I didn't mean to presume to know what kind of person you'd be interested in. I was just concerned."

"My calendar is filled just fine. Besides, I never listen to anyone else's opinion. I find it better to get to know people myself. Many times, others give you their views because they have some kind of motive."

"I've seen lots of guys hurt by Abby and I didn't want you to be one." Catherine tried to explain her actions.

"Why is it your business if I get hurt?"

"It's really not," Catherine admitted.

He laughed. "I'm flattered."

"Flattered?" she questioned with a confused look.

"That you are so concerned about my well-being," he reiterated. "But rest assured I won't be seeing Abby again. My main interest is you at the moment. Last time you mentioned that you lost your job."

"Teaching Assistant, yes." Catherine straightened. "I was cutting construction paper for the Art teacher and got sent to the Principal's office. According to Mrs. Kendawitz, the Art teacher, I was supposed to be cutting circles and I cut squares. She just said cut the paper in a shape. I thought she meant for me to pick the shape that they should be cut in. I picked the square shape, she wanted them all cut in a shape of a circle."

"Square is a fine shape."

"I completely agree with you," Catherine said. "Square is a fine shape. It's my favorite in fact."

"You got fired over such a small mistake?" Dr. Newport was feeding off of her chemistry for him. He was enjoying the fact she couldn't take her eyes off of him. Her eyes were dancing over his white suit, navy shirt and satin white tie.

"I did tell Mrs. Kendawitz to stick these squares where the sun doesn't shine."

He smiled again. "That might get a person fired then. Are you interested in obtaining another career?"

Catherine nodded yes. "I'm not sure being a teaching assistant is really my cup of tea. I do need a good job though, especially one with benefits."

"Not into cutting circles anymore." He jotted that down on his paper. "Perhaps you might want to check down the street at the Local Employment Office. It's Tuesday and they update in the mornings. Janet Dunbar is a friend of one of my secretaries." He reached into his jacket and handed her a card for Janet Dunbar, Senior Job Search Executive.

"This could be quite helpful." Catherine thanked him.

"You'll need a good job if you are still planning to move out of your boyfriend's."

"So, you could tell that Lucky was abusive?" Catherine asked.

"Let's stay focused on you right now. You are my patient, not him. I want to make sure that you stay positive and progress both mentally and physically." The doctor stood. "Has anyone ever talked to you before about how daily exercise can help some of the symptoms of depression and anxiety?"

"You're putting me on a fitness plan?" Catherine rolled her eyes. "I'm fine with my weight, really."

"I'm concerned about your anxiety and your self-esteem too."

"Do I look that bad?" Catherine asked him.

"Do you look as good as you can?" he threw back.

"I don't need to be reminded that I have a pretty face; if I just lost weight, I would be okay looking," Catherine said.

"So, you are fine overweight," he stated matter-of-factly. "Could that be because you're using the extra weight as a safety net?"

"What?"

"Maybe this goes even deeper. You don't want men to find you attractive, so you'll have an excuse to stay with Lucky," the doctor stated. "You are using food to handle stress?"

He was getting to her. By the watering of her gray eyes, he could tell.

Her hands started trembling. "I'll be sure to speak to Ms. Dunbar. Now can I have that prescription for refills?"

"Leaving, already?"

"I should get to that employment office before all the best jobs get taken," she said.

He printed out a prescription, signed the bottom and handed it to her. "I'll need to see you next month for the next refill. I want to make sure you continue to have no side effects. Some women gain weight on this medicine and since you don't seem interested in maintaining a good fitness plan, I want to keep an eye on you."

Wiping back tears, Catherine moved toward the door.

"Catherine," he said, "just so you know. Regardless of what Abby said about your appearance, Will told me he thought you were 'a Greek Goddess'. Even though men still might find you good looking overweight, I'm not going to let you hide your true self anymore. It is not working, at least not with me."

She turned to find him directly behind her. Catherine gasped in disbelief. "Will said I was a Greek Goddess?"

"We've got a lot of work to do, Catherine," the doctor said. "Rome wasn't built in one day. I'll see you next month."

CHAPTER 19

Catherine walked into the Employment Office and approached the svelte middle aged brunette woman standing behind a counter. For a minute the woman completely ignored her by speaking into a cell phone. Finally, she held up an index finger for Catherine to wait a little longer. At least she was finally being addressed.

Catherine went through her purse and pulled out the card Dr. Newport had given her. After several more minutes, she held the card out to the woman who was still, in her opinion, being rude.

Immediately, the woman hung up. "Good morning. I'm sorry to have kept you waiting." She put her cell phone down under the desk. "That was my niece. She's pregnant and not feeling well today."

"I'm sorry to hear that." Catherine smiled.

"How can I help you?"

"Dr. Newport gave me this card. He said that Janet Dunbar could help me find a job."

"What exactly are you looking for? Do you have any particular skills?"

"I type 74 words per minute. I've been a receptionist before for about six years and just recently got fired as a teacher's assistant."

"What happened?" the woman asked.

Catherine looked down at her name tag. "Stacy, I can't seem to cut construction paper into the right shape."

Stacy flipped back her brown hair and pulled down her glasses. "Fired over construction paper?"

"Yes, the good thing was I realized I'm not…" She stressed these words. "…cut out to be a Teacher's Assistant. I think I prefer being a secretary of some kind. Do you think I can make an appointment with Ms. Dunbar?"

"Janet isn't in today." Stacy suddenly grinned. "But I know the perfect job for you, and I haven't even posted on our internet site yet. No one knows of it so you'd be the first person to apply."

"What kind of job?"

Stacy went through a cabinet and then pulled out a file. She hurried through a few pages and yanked one out. "Here it is. Castle Builders of the Great States is hiring a new receptionist. That's not far from here, just about a half a mile down Eastwood Trail."

"I know where Eastwood Trail is."

Stacy continued to read. "You apply online or by fax. They recommend you list how you heard of the job. You better put down that you were recommended for the job by Janet Dunbar. They know her there."

"But I've never met Janet." Catherine raised a brow.

"I'll let Janet know you'll be using her as a reference. Janet won't mind at all. We do this all the time. This is really a great job. They have medical, dental and 401K! Starting pay is near twenty-two dollars an hour."

Catherine gasped. "Twenty-two dollars an hour!"

"You're dealing with commercial real estate brokers, privately financed home builders. We're talking the elite. Castle Builders is looking for a person who types well, can answer several phone lines, take messages, and who looks and acts completely professional." Stacy glanced down at Catherine's dress.

"I could buy some fancy business suits with that kind of pay," Catherine reassured. "Is it full time?"

"Paid holidays, sick time and two weeks paid vacation starting the first year. Let's see, it's Monday-Friday, ten to four, with one hour for lunch right in the business district."

"Those are easy hours." Catherine's eyes widened.

"Castle Builders of the Great States is that big four-story building right behind Sam's sub shop."

Extremely interested in the position, she inquired, "Can I fill out the application here?"

Stacy went around the desk and handed her two pages. "Fill this out at one of our stations and I'll fax it right to Castle Builders this afternoon. Don't forget to list Janet Dunbar as how you heard of the job."

Catherine took the paper and walked over to a round table. She fumbled through her purse and grabbed a pen. Right next to the line, "How did you find out about this job," Catherine scribbled the name, "Janet Dunbar."

Her pen trembled a bit while she wrote it. She was afraid, perhaps, of never meeting a woman and using her as a reference. This job was too great to pass up, however. The hours were perfect, and it wasn't far from Dr. Newport's office.

She filled out all the lines, even the ones she didn't like, like her current address and that her last job was that of a Teaching Assistant. She didn't dare put down that they should contact them. After all, being fired over construction paper didn't seem very prestigious.

Once she was finished, she reread the application, checking to make sure that she hadn't made any errors. She put down a few coworkers for references from her receptionist job. They would give her a great recommendation. She had worked there over six years before moving to this part of Florida.

Catherine stood and approached Stacy who was again on the phone. This time Stacy hung up the second she saw her standing there. "All done?" Stacy asked.

"Are you sure I should have put down Janet's name?" Catherine showed her that she had listed her.

"I just got off the phone and found out that it was fine," Stacy said. "It's all ready to be faxed then," Catherine said.

Stacy looked over the resume then walked over to the fax machine. She put the paper in a slot, dialed a number, and watched as it slowly was read through. Once it was completed, there was a beeping noise.

"It went through okay," Stacy announced.

"Thanks." Catherine replaced her pen in her purse. "So, are there any other jobs that I should apply for?"

"Why don't you wait and see if Castle Builders calls," suddenly Stacy took the Castle Builders of the Great States folder and stuffed it in the trash, "especially since you'll be the only one applying."

"You shouldn't do that." Catherine smiled tightly.

"For Dr. Newport, I'd do just about anything." Stacy grinned. "Do you know what his nickname is?"

"No, what?"

"Doctor Hot-Stuff," Stacy informed.

"You're kidding?" Catherine snickered.

"All the female counselors call him that behind his back and he doesn't even know."

"Really?"

"And you should see his friends, too, Will and Stanley! They are all so gorgeous!"

Catherine began to turn away but then proudly added, "I know Will, too. You're right. They are both really handsome men."

Stacy raised her ring finger, flashing a large diamond ring which sparkled from the sun coming in from the window. "If I wasn't married, I sure would have tried for a few house calls from that doctor, believe me!"

Catherine walked out the door, smiling. For the first time in a long time, she felt as if there was hope. She was glad she wasn't the only one who found Dr. Newport so breathtakingly beautiful. Nor could she forget Dr. Newport telling her about Will's compliment. Will had called her a Greek Goddess. That was the nicest thing anyone ever said about her.

CHAPTER 20

Catherine walked to a pay phone outside of the Employment Office and dialed a familiar number. After two rings, she checked her watch. It was too early for her mother to have left for bingo.

"Hello."

"Mom, it's me. I'm on the corner of Third and Andrews; can you pick me up?" Catherine questioned.

"Are you okay?" She immediately worried. "Did Lucky hurt you?"

"No!" Catherine reassured. "I have something else to talk to you about. Besides wouldn't it be nice to spend the afternoon together before you go off to the center to play tonight?"

"Sounds fun," her mother said. "Let me get my purse and put on some make-up and I'll be on my way. Don't go anywhere."

"I'll be on the corner of Third," Catherine promised and then hung up.

She waited by the street on a bench not far from a bus stop. A motorcycle pulled up nearby and Catherine didn't dare look up at the man who sat down next to her. All she could tell is that he was huge, muscular, and by the huge Indian chief tattoo, more than likely Native American.

"Good afternoon," he said.

Catherine turned her body in the opposite direction, making it very clear she was not going to speak to strangers. She didn't respond.

Maybe she should go back to the employment office and wait until her mother drove up in her car. She thought if there were motorcycle gang members around here that might be a safer choice.

"You wouldn't happen to know Blake Anderson, would you?" he asked.

The name sounded familiar, but Catherine couldn't place where she had heard of it. "No. Please leave me alone, or I'll call the police."

A chuckle came from the stranger, deep and low. His long black braid flipped over one shoulder as he rose and in a low voice said, "You do that."

Catherine watched him get onto his motorcycle and start the engine. He was absolutely enormous. Chills ran through her spine. Very glad he had decided to leave on his own, she took a sigh of relief.

It didn't take very long for her mother to pull up in her minivan and unlock the door for Catherine to enter. She immediately rushed around the vehicle and climbed up on the one step to sit in the passenger's side.

"Hi." Catherine grinned.

"Hi, Sweetie. Spill the beans. What's going on? I can tell by that shit-eating grin of yours that you are up to something."

"I am." Catherine's smile grew.

"It doesn't require me to sell anything for bond money, does it?"

"No, Mom." Catherine laughed. "I applied for a really great front desk job."

Her mother's face showed her approval. Then as soon as the happiness raised her spirits, a shadow lowered her eyes and puckered her lips. "You haven't told Lucky about wanting a job, have you?"

"No," Catherine admitted.

"He won't like it."

"I know." Catherine sighed. "It's just it seemed like such a good idea when Doctor Newport suggested it."

"Doctor Newport?" Her mother pulled the minivan over to park. "You went to see him again?"

"Yes." Catherine shrugged. "Why did you pull over?"

"Snack attack." Her mother pointed to the store they were parked in front of, THE CHOCOLATE DREAMER. On the outside was a sign which read, "Buy one half pound of candy, get the second FREE. Chocolate covered bananas ½ price."

"Mom, I'm trying to lose weight," Catherine reminded.

"Can't even talk you into a banana? Bananas are a fruit."

"One." Catherine's stomach was practically growling at just the thought of the scrumptious treat. "That's it!"

They both exited the minivan and sat down at a table outside underneath a large umbrella with candy canes on top. Catherine picked up the menu and scanned over all the different kinds of desserts they could order. Her mouth was watering as the waitress approached to take their order.

"I'll have one chocolate covered banana," Catherine said.

"I'll have one half pound of dipped strawberries and a scoop of chocolate ice cream covered in fudge on the side," her mother informed the waitress.

After the young woman had jotted down their order, she asked, "Would you both like nuts?"

"Nut free," Catherine said.

"Nuts are fine with me," her mother agreed. "Crushed peanuts or almond slices."

"Peanuts on top of the ice cream," her mother said. "Plus bring us some bottled waters. Make it snappy, Little Lady. I don't have all day to snap on a feed bag."

The waitress laughed as she walked away. "Coming right up."

"So," her mother returned her attention back to her daughter, "what else did this Doctor Newport say?"

"Like I said he thought it would be a good idea if I got a job and become more independent. He gave me a name at the Employment Office, and I went down there and applied for a job."

"Good for Newport," her mother praised. "I think I like that man."

"You've never even met him."

"He cares about your sense of self," her mother said.

"Why do you say that?"

"He is thinking about what's best for you. He knows that you are in a relationship which is very controlling."

"I hope I can even do this job." Catherine grimaced.

"You can do anything you set your mind to," her mother reminded her. "I've always believed in you."

"I think I want to become an astronaut or maybe a major league baseball player then."

"Okay, maybe you can't achieve everything you dream of." Her mother's eyes grew with pleasure as the waitress brought out their desserts on a tray. "But within reason, shoot for the moon."

CHAPTER 21

"I can't believe Hayden went right up to her," Fred snipped to Blake, lowering his binoculars. "He is such a jerk. He's trying to blow our cover."

"Forget about cover." Blake smiled. "I want a chocolate covered banana like Catherine."

"Stay put." Fred coughed.

"Are you sick, dude?" Blake questioned. "You keep coughing."

Fred wiped the sweat from his brow. "My wife had the flu last week and I might have caught a bit of it. I'm all right, though."

"I can't catch that." Blake sat back in the passenger's side of the sedan. "I got the games coming up."

"Is that all you think about?"

"Dude, it's what I live for. This P.I. stuff is how I make my money so I can do what I do and travel."

"Are you really that good at skateboarding?" Fred inquired. "Our secretary went on and on about some competition you were in last year."

"I prefer snowboarding over skateboarding, but my favorite vice is surfing over everything else," Blake confessed. "There is just something about being on a board in the ocean. It makes you feel like it's just you and the Big Man upstairs. You really feel small and at His mercy. However, when you catch that perfect wave, it's like harmony or something."

"That was deep." Fred rolled his eyes.

"Seriously, can't I just sneak in behind the women and get us some chocolate covered bananas? They'll never see me."

"After what Hayden just pulled, I don't think so," Fred reminded. "The last thing we need is for Catherine Walters to figure out she's under surveillance."

"Don't you find it odd that Hayden keeps showing up?" Blake commented. "It's almost like the undercover cops are watching us, watch her."

"You're being ridiculous now!"

"No, seriously, dude," Blake argued. "I have a feeling they want to know why we are putting her under surveillance."

"Hayden just wants to stick it to Cilva." Fred tossed the binoculars on the dashboard. "They have this agreement to hate each other."

"Hate is a strong word." Blake sighed. "Why would Hayden be so curious if he didn't think the boss was onto something with this Catherine chick?"

Fred took a moment to ponder on Blake's comments. His eyes stayed glued to Catherine and her mother who were now halfway finished with their desserts. "You want one too, don't you?" Blake laughed. "That banana sure would hit the spot on this hot day."

"No kidding."

"It's not a big deal for me to get out, walk down the street and go into the shop behind the table. They won't even see me and then we'd have some chocolate covered bananas for all our trouble."

"Our only problem is Hayden," Fred said. "What do you think he said to Catherine?"

"Whatever it was, Catherine didn't seem too impressed with him."

"Yes," Fred agreed. "She was afraid of him."

"Bad instincts," Blake said.

"Why do you say that?" Fred wondered. "You didn't care much for the guy who keeps calling you kid."

"You're right, I don't like him but I get him."

"You do?" Fred chuckled.

"Hayden thinks he's alpha dog. He just doesn't know that I am really the big boner around these parts now."

"True." Fred laughed. "You are a big boner. I can honestly say, I completely agree with that."

"You're not understanding. Hayden doesn't hate us. He respects us enough to want to know what we do. He knows that we wouldn't be watching Catherine if it wasn't important."

"Good point." Fred nodded.

"Don't get me wrong. Whatever we are up to, he not only wants to know but also take over."

"Lucky should be in jail if he hits that pretty thing," Fred said.

"She's not bad." Blake pulled out the wallet from his side pant pocket. "Check out my girl though."

"Holy moly." Fred's eyes widened. "This young lady actually dates you. Are you sure about that?"

"She's my girlfriend," Blake said with pride.

"My goodness. That's a good-looking girlfriend you've got there." Fred then yanked out his leather wallet and flashed a picture of a middle-aged woman with two female teenagers. "This is my queen and our princesses."

"Wow, your old lady is a cutie."

"Thank you." Fred proudly glanced at his family picture. "I think so. I can't even remember a time I didn't love this woman."

"You're a family man."

"Yes, and that's why I can't stand guys like Lucky." Fred shut his wallet. "I keep thinking what if one of my daughters winds up with someone violent. They should lock these guys up."

"Does this have something to do with that Janet woman?" Blake questioned. "Does she work with our abuse cases?"

"Nice try." Fred stuffed his wallet in the glove box of the sedan and then glanced back at Catherine and her mother. "It would kill my wife if one of ours winds up in a situation like Catherine is in."

"You shouldn't worry about that too much. I bet you've warned them."

Fred nodded. "I hope I've made some impact telling them how many of these cases I've been on."

Four days later...

CHAPTER 22

Seated at the dining table, chewing on breakfast sausage next to Lucky, Catherine had almost forgotten about the application when the phone suddenly rang. Lucky put down his sharp fork eating pancakes and reached across to the kitchen counter to greet whoever was on the line.

"It's for you." He handed it to her with a suspicious expression across his face.

Catherine took the receiver. "Hello… yes, this is she." She listened as the person asked her to come in at 10:00 for an interview at Castle Builders of the Great States. "Of course, I'll be there. Who am I to speak to?" She heard the name and jotted it quickly down. "Dell Mitchum."

"Who was it," Lucky asked her, sipping on a cup of coffee. Catherine replaced the receiver and screamed with joy.

Lucky nearly fell out of his seat, spilling his drink on his shirt. "You stupid bitch!"

"Sorry." She immediately grabbed a towel and began wiping his shirt. "Take it off and I'll get out the stain."

He pushed her back so hard; she fell against the kitchen counter. "Who the hell was that calling you?"

"I have a job interview. They are hiring a new receptionist at Castle Builders, and it pays near $22.00 an hour with benefits."

He roared. "I provide for us!"

"I want to work."

He ripped off his shirt. "There is no need for you to work when I make plenty."

Catherine peeled herself off the counter. "You do so much for us. It's just I want a career of my own. It has nothing to do with how much money you make."

"Don't I give you everything you want?" He shoved the shirt underneath the sink and rubbed in some hand soap to remove the coffee stain. "I don't want you working! There's no need!"

"But I want something to do while you're gone all those days."

Lucky said, "Go out to a day spa or get your hair done like Abby's girlfriends."

"I want more than that. I want a career," Catherine pleaded. "This is a great job and I'm going to the interview."

Lucky shoved the shirt into her chest. "You ruined my favorite shirt."

Catherine ran into the bedroom and grabbed another shirt for him. "Here, I'll take that one to the cleaners. They'll be able to take out the stain."

He put on the shirt, his face still red from rage. The moment it was on, he headed for the door. "Now you've made me late for a flight. When I get back, you better not have a job! I won't have it!"

With the slam of the door, Catherine's shoulders slumped, and she started to cry. Slowly, she reached for a paper towel to wipe her tears and in her head, she remembered something Dr. Newport had said. *Rome wasn't built in one day.* Her doctor was right, Catherine concluded. She decided then to get dressed. She had a job interview to go to and no one was going to stop her from trying.

"Besides," she said to herself, "even if I go to the interview that doesn't mean I will get the job."

Catherine went into the bedroom, hurried through the closet and found a simple buttoned down navy dress she had worn to her father's funeral three years before. It was dark and gloomy, but she brightened it with a colorful neck scarf.

She dressed and put on some simple jewelry. In the mirror, she checked herself. "This looks professional enough." Quickly, she grabbed her purse and suddenly noticed that her car keys were missing.

"Lucky took my keys!"

Her hands went to the phone, and she called herself a cab. In a half hour they would be at the door, and she would just make it to the ten o'clock interview with Dell Mitchum.

She looked at herself in the mirror for almost that entire time. She messed with her hair which didn't want to curl just right. Redid her make up, then she tried on a few different types of shoes only to decide to stay with the original flats she had on.

When the doorbell rang, Catherine shot for the door. She quickly moved past the driver. "Castle Builders of the Great States on Eastwood, please," Catherine said.

"The scenic route or…"

"The fastest way," Catherine pleaded, jumping into the back of the bright yellow car.

The driver sat behind the wheel and started the engine. She knew the ride was only about fifteen minutes and checked her watch. She'd be there a few minutes early, she hoped.

"So, you work for Castle Builders?" the driver asked.

"I hope to soon," Catherine announced.

"Job interview," he moved the mirror to see her, "are you nervous?"

"I am." Catherine opened her purse and took her anxiety medication Dr. Newport had prescribed. "Thank goodness for these."

The driver kept looking in the mirror. "Miss?" he called. "We seem to be… no sorry, the black truck pulled off. I was wrong."

The cab pulled into the parking lot behind Sam's Sub shop. The four-story building looked huge compared to the smaller surrounding buildings. The pillars were marble in front of the giant doors. The cab pulled up to the front.

"Do you want me to wait?" he asked. "I could have sworn we were being followed by a black pickup truck earlier."

"No thank you. I don't know anyone with a pickup truck," Catherine said. "I'll walk home."

"That will be thirty dollars."

Catherine's mouth dropped; that was more than she was expecting. She checked in her wallet and pulled out forty. "Here, have lunch on me."

"Thanks." The driver smiled. "Good luck, Miss."

Catherine moved toward the large doors only to find two doormen to greet and open them for her. Inside there were two stairwells, an elevator and a giant desk made out of marble in the middle. Behind the desk was a young man about twenty years of age. He was bald by choice and wearing a three piece suit.

"Good morning," he greeted. "Welcome to Castle Builders of the Great States. My name is Josh. How may I be of service?"

"I have a meeting this morning with…" She forgot the name for a moment. "Mitchum, Dell Mitchum."

"Your name, please?" he asked.

"Catherine Walters."

He nodded and made a phone call. "Catherine is here to see you, Mr. Mitchum." He hung up the phone and motioned for her to sit on the lounge chair to the right. "He'll be down in a few minutes. Have a seat and a cup of coffee if you'd like. There are donuts and bagels around the corner."

"I already ate," Catherine said, seating herself on the large, cushioned chair.

Minutes passed that seemed like hours. Then the elevator doors opened and an older man stood with a cane. He was wearing a buttoned down shirt and slacks, and a very well defined hair piece which matched his gray hair. On his face was a pair of round glasses which mirrored his very plump face.

"Are you Catherine?" he asked.

Interrupting, the young man greeted behind the desk, "Good morning, this is your first meeting of the day, Catherine Walters."

"Come." He waved her into the elevator.

Catherine rushed toward the older gentleman and waited for the doors to shut. "Thank you so much for seeing me today, Mr. Mitchum."

"Please, call me Dell."

"Thank you, Dell."

"It's my pleasure." He glanced over. "Janet is a very close friend of my daughter's. You could say they were exactly alike."

Catherine suddenly felt guilty. She didn't even know Janet Dunbar and here she is helping her get a job. "That's wonderful."

"Janet is special to me, more than I can say. Of course, my daughter married a horrible louse just like Janet did."

"I'm sorry."

"My daughter, Jessica, no longer speaks to me," Dell Mitchum informed. "How can I approve of someone who hurts my own flesh and blood?" His eyes began to water, then he took a handkerchief out and quickly wiped his eyes.

"That must be very hard for you to deal with."

"It affects the entire family," he said. "No one thinks of that, but it does. Thank goodness for Janet. Janet helped my daughter get a job but it was still too late to save our relationship."

"How horrible for you," Catherine said. The elevator doors opened into an incredible giant office of mahogany furniture and endless bookshelves filled with building designs. The walls were covered in artwork by Vincent VanGogh.

"This is an amazing office," Catherine said.

"My space, my Dear." Dell Mitchum slowly moved in to sit behind the desk. "Come have a seat."

Catherine sat in the chair opposite of the desk. She waited until he had shuffled through some papers before speaking again.

"Your office is spectacular, Sir. Is it one of your designs?"

"One of millions of fantastic ideas that our interior design department created. I can assure you we have a multitude of talent here." He grabbed her application and began looking it over. "Let's hope you'll be one of my talented people. I see here you were a secretary for a landscaping company for six years."

"Yes, I'm an excellent typist. I'm very good at taking messages, scheduling appointments and handling busy phone lines."

Dell Mitchum's eyes began to water again. He wiped them and put down her paper. "It's hard for me when I meet friends of Janet's. It just reminds me of Jessica, and I… know…" He wiped his eyes again. "Why am I bothering you with my personal life? You are kind to listen to an old man's problems."

"It's no bother, Mister—"

"Aw-aw." He held up a finger and shook it at her. His animated smile removed any trace of seriousness censure. "Dell, remember?"

"I remember." She gave him a demure smile.

"Good. You're hired, Catherine. You start Monday morning at ten. Go see the lobby attendant for all the information on your job. That bald kid will have all the paperwork. He works the night shift and hates getting up before ten. He'll be very pleased that you'll be joining us."

"You won't be sorry you hired me!" Catherine smiled and shook his hand.

"Baldy is Josh by the way. He's my nephew, a real pain, but he's always on time as long as he works the night shifts."

"Thank you so much, Dell. I looked forward to working at the front desk."

"Go downstairs and tell Josh to have you fill out the employee benefit papers. That will get you started for the day shift on Monday." Dell winked. "Welcome to my staff. You'll find a comfortable home here."

CHAPTER 23

Driving his convertible sports car, Jay spoke into his cell phone. "Thank you for rescheduling my morning appointments, Margie. I can't believe I slept through my alarm. If you hadn't rung my house earlier, I would still be sleeping. I had a late night with a great spy novel."

"Don't worry, Doctor," replied the familiar voice of his loyal secretary. She had rescheduled most of his appointments for next week.

"I'll be in shortly. I'm going to stop by Sam's subs and pick us up some lunch."

"Thank you, Dr. Newport. See you soon." As she hung up, Jay saw Catherine out of the corner of his eye. He blinked as if he couldn't believe it. He closed his cell phone as his mouth dropped open and he watched her sashay down the street.

"Wow," he said, gazing at her in the navy suit, her dark curly hair bouncing in the breeze as it reflected the shimmering sun. "She certainly knows how to put herself together."

He waited until he got to the next street and then whirled his convertible around to see where she was headed. A truck horn came from behind and from his side view mirror, Jay saw Will's black pickup truck.

He waved the truck to pull alongside. The pickup's window slid down and Will shouted, "How'd you escape the office?"

"I slept in."

"Fred caught the flu so I'm covering Catherine today. So far it looks like she landed that Castle Builders of the Great States job."

As both vehicles slowly turned the corner, the doctor found Catherine walking up the stairs into a large wooden white church at the end of the street.

Why is she going in there? Jay wondered.

Will parked half a block down from the church. Jay pulled his car around the truck and parked on the side street to exit his vehicle. Will remained in his truck with the window rolled down.

"Jay, what are you doing?" Will pulled out a newspaper and opened it to hide his face. "Catherine could come out of the church any minute."

The doctor stood beside the truck. "Did you see how different she looked, even the way she walked? Confident!"

"Catherine's a knockout, all right." Will folded the paper down. "I could see through the side window of their house, Lucky rough handle her this morning. Shoved her against the kitchen counter."

"Lucky doesn't want her working," the doctor guessed.

"I agree. She looks like a new person," Will commented.

"Until she goes home. Lucky isn't going to like her going against his wishes." The doctor turned toward the church. "I want to see what she's doing."

Will cautioned him, "Don't blow our cover."

"I'll be right back."

"I thought you didn't like religious places," Will said.

"Religion keeps the masses from committing crimes."

"Coming from a Catholic, Doc, your views on religion can be a little on the offensive side."

"Why is my opinion any more offensive than yours?"

"You're getting off the subject, Jay. And I know why. You're trying to stop me from seeing how important Catherine is becoming to you. This is getting too personal for you, my friend."

Jay shook his head in disagreement and hurried toward the small white church. The front doors stood open. He slowly moved up the steps and quietly stood in the doorway. He found Catherine alone, kneeling at the altar.

With tears falling, she clasped her hands and started to pray aloud. "Dear God, please don't let anything happen to me when I tell Lucky I got hired."

It was all he could do not to rush over to comfort her. He took a couple steps inside and stood there listening. As she leaned forward and lit a single white candle, he made sure she didn't see his shadow on the side wall.

She continued, her eyes closing. "Give me strength when I tell him." His hands started shaking. The doctor wanted badly to talk to her.

"Whatever happens, I love you, Jesus. I know you would want more for me than someone who hurts or puts me down. Thank you for protecting me this morning and not letting things get even worse. And thank you for bringing Dr. Jay Newport into my life to help me. It's nice having someone to talk to."

He heard a honk and knew it was Cilva warning him not to go further in. Just as her hands unclasped from in front of her, the doctor turned and rushed out the door and down the street.

He ran over to Will's truck and grabbed him by the sleeve of his shirt. "If Lucky so much as lays one more hand on her, I want to know it!"

Will gasped, glancing down at the hand clutching his garment. "Jay?"

"Did you hear me? I want to know immediately!"

"Whatever you want."

"Immediately!"

It's on your bill; just remember that."

"Don't let Lucky get close to hurting her again. Figure out a way to stop him. Ring the doorbell! Break down the door! I don't give a damn how you protect her, just do whatever is necessary!"

"Jay, it's going to be all right." Will tried to alleviate his friend's worry.

"I'm not worried about me," the doctor said and sneered.

"I've never seen you like this before."

"Just do what I pay you for! Protect her." The doctor rushed away to his car. Immediately, he got behind the wheel and peeled out, leaving rubber on the street.

Just as his vehicle turned the corner, Catherine walked out of the church, wiping tears off her cheeks. Will raised the newspaper again so she wouldn't see him behind the truck's wheel.

CHAPTER 24

In Dr. Newport's office, Catherine sat across his desk from him, more nervous than usual. Her eyes were still watery from her visit to the church. He straightened in his chair, trying hard not to show how happy he was she had decided to stop by and talk her fears out with him.

"Thank you for seeing me on such short notice," she finally murmured.

"Normally, I don't take walk-ins, but I had a cancellation, so it works out good for both of us. I had just finished eating my lunch when my secretary told me you were out front and upset."

"You have no idea how happy I am that you could make time to see me." Catherine took a tissue from her purse, wiping her eyes.

Jay handed her the entire box he kept on his desk. "Now, tell me what's going on, Catherine?"

"I went for a job interview today at Castle Builders of the Great States and they hired me. I start on Monday." She smiled through her tears.

"That's fantastic news!"

"The card you gave me really helped. Stacy at the Employment office told me to put Janet Dunbar's name down as a reference on my application. Once the boss, Dell Mitchum, saw her name, I was hired."

"You're giving Janet too much credit. You wouldn't have gotten the job if you couldn't handle the responsibilities."

Catherine appreciated the compliment. "I never thought of that."

"So, if it's not your new employment status…" Jay closed his laptop, put it aside, giving her his full attention instead of taking notes as he would normally do "What's wrong?"

"I'm afraid of going home."

"Your boyfriend or husband? I'm sorry, which was it?" He pretended to not recall. "I remember meeting him. What was his name again?"

"Lucky, and he's been my boyfriend for about two years."

"That's right, the airplane pilot. You're trying to break off things with him."

"Yes, and it's a great thing he's a pilot. He's off again to the Bahamas, taking some men on a business trip. He'll be back in two days." Catherine sighed. "I don't know how to tell Lucky that I did get this job. He was really against me working, and I am worried that he won't take the news well."

"When you say, 'he won't take it well,' what you really mean is, he may become violent. Isn't that correct?" Jay focused on the gray gems of her eyes, still sparkling with tears.

"Yes, Doc."

"Then the solution is simple."

"Please, tell me what to do," Catherine pleaded. "I really need your advice."

"Don't tell him," The Doctor said.

"But that's lying," Catherine put forth.

"You're hiding the truth to save yourself from a beating. I would say it's justified." Dr. Newport began jotting some information down on her file on the desk. "How is your anxiety?"

"Worsening," Catherine admitted.

"I'm going to prescribe a very low dosage of Valium, just a few pills. In the next few days to aid your anti-depressive anxiety medication; take as needed."

Catherine nodded with a smile. "Okay."

"This isn't something you'll require on a regular basis. Just take one while you're going through a lot of extra stress."

"I don't like lying to Lucky."

"Do you have your own bank account?" he asked.

"We have a joint one."

"When you start your new job, go down to another bank and put money away every paycheck. Before long you'll have enough to get your own apartment."

Catherine whimpered. "I'm so scared."

"Living on your own is a frightening thing." Jay understood, from his own experience. "When I went away to college, I was so homesick I called my mom every night for the first three months. One time I even packed my bags and went home."

"You!" Catherine chuckled. "I don't believe it."

The doctor grinned. "My mother took one look at this college boy mess and told me to get back to school. She yelled at me that she didn't pay all that tuition for nothing! I was so hurt I begged her to let me stay home. She called a cab, and I started to cry right in the middle of our driveway. When the cab finally got there, my mom opened the door and told me to think of her as a mother bird and I was her little baby she was kicking out of the nest. She said, 'I love you enough I want you to fly on your own.'"

Catherine wiped at her sympathetic tears. "That's a very touching story, Doc."

"You have to do this on your own, Catherine. You have to face your fears and that doesn't mean telling Lucky. It means doing what's best for you. Think of yourself first, not him. If you have to protect yourself then do it. Do what you have to, and I will support you one hundred percent."

"I've never lived on my own before. After my father died, I met Lucky and moved to this side of the state."

"You've got enough smarts to handle being on your own."

"No one has ever said that to me before," Catherine admitted. "I've always thought of myself as not very intelligent."

"You're chock full of brains, Catherine." He picked up the laptop again and made another quick note. "Your self-esteem is the real issue. I believe Lucky has had a hand in insulting you to the point you started believing the things he says about you."

"He claims I'm hopeless, stupid and lazy."

"Turn things around. Think to yourself that the only dumb decision you made was to be with a man who thinks nothing of hurting you, both physically and mentally. You have a job now. You are a woman who puts herself together quite nicely." He glanced up and down at her navy dress. "If Lucky was smart, he'd realize what he has in you and stop acting like a jerk!"

Catherine stood, taking the prescription. "You always make me feel so good about myself."

The doctor shook her hand, smiling. "Don't worry, Catherine. You're on the right track."

"Thank you for all your advice, Doc."

"If you need me, call."

"I'm putting you on speed dial."

Catherine walked out the door with a grin planted on her face.

CHAPTER 25

Catherine walked to her mother's house. Her head was filled with the hope that Lucky would never find out that she'd gotten a job with Castle Builders of America. She was so happy and terrified, all at the same time.

Knocking on her mother's door, she waited outside. A small mockingbird was feeding from a sunflower seed birdfeeder not far from the palm landscaping which was blossoming with pansies.

The door swung open, and her mother stood in a long pink and white bathrobe and matching fluffy slippers. "Hi, Honey."

"Mom? What are you wearing?"

"You like? I saw this ensemble at the mall and couldn't resist."

"Interesting." Catherine's eyes focused on her mother's feet which were almost invisible underneath the pink fuzz.

"I just thought, why not?"

Catherine wondered if this impulse buy had anything to do with the fact her operation was later next week. "As long as you like pink fuzzy things. That's all that counts." She checked her watch. "It's almost noon. Aren't you going to get dressed today?"

"Nope." Her mother ushered her inside the house where all the curtains were shut tight.

"You're not going to get dressed?"

"I decided that today I am doing nothing. I am going to sit on the couch, watch a few movies and eat everything bad for me I can possibly think of."

Catherine glanced over at the sofa through the darkness. Next to the remote was a pile of cheese puffs, two hot dogs and chocolate cake. "You're off to a great start for ruining my diet."

"Would you like to join me in hiding away from the world today?"

"I suppose I could," Catherine admitted. "I just came back from Doctor Newport's office and Lucky is still flying a crew to the Bahamas."

"Perfect!" Her mother sat back down. "I have several movies for you to choose from. I tried to pick the hottest stars wearing the least clothing as possible."

"You're trying not to think about that operation, right?" Catherine understood. Her mother didn't answer while handing Catherine several DVD boxes. "I've seen a few of these."

"Pick any one with Paul Walker, McConaughey, or Johnny Depp half naked." Catherine grabbed the Lone Ranger DVD and waited until her mother had popped it into the DVD player.

"I had a good session."

"With Dr. Newport?" her mother inquired.

"It was very promising. He seemed to really understand my situation with Lucky and gave me some advice on how to tell him the news."

"What news?" Her mother's eyes widened, as though she were puzzled.

"That I got the job with Castle Builders of America!"

Her mother stood up and grabbed Catherine around the shoulders in a big, congratulatory embrace. The hug lasted a few moments, and as Catherine pulled back to relax, she noticed the tears falling from her mother's cheeks.

"Mom?"

"I'm so proud of you."

"It's just a job," Catherine said.

"No, it's the job you wanted," her mother pointed out. "I remember how you told me the doctor gave you a card at the employment office. You wanted this job so badly!"

"Yes, I got the job because of Janet Dunbar knowing owner Dell Mitchum. Apparently, Janet knew his daughter."

Her mother grabbed a tissue from off the coffee table and wiped her face clear of tears. "That's wonderful."

"I don't know much about them. All I know is Mr. Mitchum is very sad about his relationship with his daughter. She married someone he didn't approve of and now they are estranged."

"That's awful," her mother sympathized.

"I got the feeling Mr. Mitchum is devastated that his daughter is with this person. Janet is a friend that's helped him through this, I suppose."

"Is there anything you can do?"

"I don't even know Janet Dunbar," Catherine confessed. "The woman at the Employment office told me to put her name down as a reference. I felt kind of weird about it and almost didn't do it."

"I'm sure you got the job because you can do the job, not just who you know," her mother reminded.

"I hope so because I honestly don't know this Janet person and I would hate for Mr. Mitchum to ever find out."

"When do you start?"

"Monday," Catherine said. "I have to hide it from Lucky though."

"I don't think that's a good idea," her mother advised. "Lucky has a lot of friends. What if one of them knows someone at Castle Builders of America? That could put you in a hairy spot."

"I'm just not going to mention it."

"Is that what Doctor Newport told you to do?" her mother inquired. "Is that his brain buster?"

"That was what he suggested."

"Just go to work and Lucky not have a clue where you are? I give that a day at the most before Lucky starts wondering why you are gone so long," her mother said. "You need to rethink this approach."

"What do you suggest?"

"Be honest," her mother said.

"He'll get very angry."

"Tell Lucky quickly and get out of the house until he calms down. You can even leave him a note and spend the night here. By morning maybe, he will have gotten it in his head that you are employed," her mother added.

"That's not a bad idea."

"It's better. I'm not quite sure the doctor understands that at times Lucky becomes violent."

"I told the doctor," Catherine admitted.

"You did?" Her mother started the movie, then reached down and began opening a bag of cheese curls. "You are opening up to him, aren't you?"

"I know." Catherine smiled, leaning back to watch the upcoming feature in black and white. "I trust him. And his advice."

CHAPTER 26

Catherine spent the next few days cleaning the house, ironing and watching television. She kept herself busy, waiting anxiously for Lucky to arrive from his piloting trip back from the Bahamas.

When the front door finally opened, Catherine greeted Lucky with open arms.

He received her with a quick kiss and a hug. "Miss me?"

"Of course," she replied, matter-of-factly. They parted as he went up the stairs with a suitcase. Her eyes trailed after him, waiting patiently for the question she knew was coming.

"You didn't go to that interview, right?"

"You didn't want me to," she reminded him.

"Good." He headed into the bedroom.

She went to the sofa and turned on the television. An hour passed as she listened to the sounds of him taking a shower and then fumbling around the closet to get dressed. He came downstairs in a bathing suit and clutching a towel.

"Let's swim," he ordered and then he opened the patio door, heading outside to the pool.

Catherine hurried upstairs and changed into a one piece lavender bathing suit. Looking at herself in the mirror, she couldn't help but feel insecure about the extra weight around her middle. Hurrying, she went downstairs and into the moonlight. Lucky had turned on the pool lights and was in a floating lounge chair listening to music.

"Wow, you look fat," he said, coldly.

"I've started on a diet," she admitted. He jumped off the chair as she slowly entered the pool. Instead of stopping by her side, he went up the stairs to the phone on the wall and dialed a number, pounding his fingers on the numbers.

"Castle Builders of the Great States?" he asked. "My girlfriend Catherine Walters is starting on Monday. What time is she supposed to be there?"

Catherine's breath caught in her throat.

"That's her, the new receptionist at the front desk. When does she start?" Lucky asked, coldly. "Thank you so much. I'll be sure to tell her."

She saw hatred in his eyes as he slammed down the phone and jumped into the water. Swimming as fast as she could, she tried desperately to get to the metal ladder in the deep end, but his cold, large hands clutched around her ankles, yanking her down into the deep.

The air came from her lungs, bubbling upward as she struggled to get to the surface. Suddenly he pulled her up. "Lucky," she said and coughed. "Let me go!"

Instead of granting her wish, Lucky thrust her down into the water again. This time she faced him as she struggled, pushing him away from her. He would not let go of her arms no matter how much she scratched at his chest.

Then suddenly he gave her another chance for air. As soon as his head was out of the water, BANG, came sound of a gunshot. The bullet whizzed past Lucky's head. Lucky released her and jumped out of the pool, searching where the bullet had been shot from.

Catherine struggled to get out of the pool. She coughed up water and lay down on her side on the cement, coughing and trying to catch her breath.

"Who shot at me?" Lucky screamed.

"What?" she gasped.

"There was someone up here with a gun!" Lucky roared. "Who the hell... he was tall... who was he?"

"I don't know!"

Lucky ran for the house and Catherine got up and wrapped a towel around her body. Barely able to stand, she stumbled for the gate. Someone grabbed her, she wasn't sure who. He picked her up and tossed her into the back of a black pickup truck.

She struggled to roll over to see who was now behind the wheel, but his back was turned to her. He had brown hair that came down to his shoulders. Her head went back down to rest on her hands. She needed to catch her breath.

"Stay down!" he yelled.

Catherine didn't argue. Instead, her hands curled together and she quietly mumbled, "Thank you, Jesus." After speaking the last word, everything seemed to spin, and blackness came and took her.

* * * *

Catherine woke up in a hospital bed, tubes coming out of her arms and her head propped up on a pillow. No one was in the room. She wasn't sure if she was dreaming at first, for the last thing she remembered was being in the back seat of a black truck and not being able to see who the driver was.

Her throat felt sore from coughing. She rubbed her neck and noticed the needle in her arm attached to an IV stand. If she had felt better, it would have disgusted her, but now she hadn't the strength to complain. In fact, she concluded, she was exactly where she needed to be.

The hospital room door opened and in walked a man wearing a white coat. His name tag was blocked by his arm holding up a chart. "Good morning, Catherine," he greeted. "My name is Doctor Kerry Douglas. I was your ER Doctor when you were brought in for nearly drowning. Do you remember talking to me?"

"No," she said. "How long have I been admitted?"

"Since last night. The police have already been here," he informed. "They stopped by your residency and obtained paperwork for your insurance information. They said the man who opened the door was covered in scratches."

Catherine suddenly asked, "Is it Monday?"

"Sunday morning."

"Good," she said and sighed. "I have to get to work tomorrow. I'm starting a new job."

"I'm not sure you'll be released, Catherine," the doctor informed. "I need to run a few more tests to make sure you don't have any permanent brain damage."

"I'm fine," Catherine said. "I don't want to talk to the police and whatever you do don't call my mother. She's going through enough right now. I can't have her see me all bruised like this."

"Officer Baker just wanted to ask you some questions about what happened. You, certainly, want to put whoever made those marks on your arms behind bars, right?"

Catherine looked down at her arms and chest and saw the black and blue marks. The last thing she wanted was to make Lucky any angrier than what he already was now that she was employed.

"I don't want to talk to the police," she said.

"You may not have a choice…" Dr. Douglas turned, hearing the door, and found Dr. Jay Newport standing there. "Morning, Jay, I wasn't aware she was a patient of yours."

"I was alerted last night that one of my patients had been admitted under distress," he quickly explained. "How is Catherine doing?"

"I have a few more tests to run but overall, the outlook is good and she can be released in the next few days."

Catherine alerted. "I start work tomorrow, Doc."

"I'm sure your boss will understand your being in the hospital," Dr. Newport replied.

"It's my first day," Catherine said. "I can't miss it."

Dr. Newport began studying the black and blue marks on her arms. "This Lucky's doing?"

Catherine gasped, "I don't want to talk to the police."

Dr. Douglas immediately informed, "They have been here already, Jay."

"Officer Baker?" Dr. Newport inquired.

"They sent Janet Baker, all right," Dr. Douglas informed.

Doctor Jay Newport leaned over her. "Let me see what I can do about you talking." He grinned with his brilliant white teeth. "You look good for a woman who was almost murdered."

"I'm fine," Catherine told him. "Who brought me in? I don't remember much of what happened."

Dr. Newport stepped back from the bed. "Can I speak to you for a moment, Dr. Douglas?" He motioned for the door.

"Certainly," he replied.

The two men exited the hospital room, leaving Catherine with more questions than answers.

CHAPTER 27

Catherine waited, but Dr. Newport didn't return to her hospital room. Later in the day, she was released by Dr. Douglas. She was placed in a wheelchair and taken to a taxicab outside. Slowly, she got in behind the driver, wearing nothing but the bathing suit and towel.

"Mall," she informed the driver, clutching her purse.

With a quick nod, Catherine sat back into the cab and didn't say a word until he pulled up to SHARRON'S FASHION, which was the largest store at the west end of the mall. "Stop right here."

"Twenty-five dollars," he announced, parking the vehicle.

Catherine opened her purse and her wallet. There was nothing inside. "Oh, no. I had fifty dollars in here." She fumbled through her wallet and found that all of the credit cards that Lucky had given her were gone.

How would she rent a motel room? Where would she spend the night? How could she buy an outfit for work tomorrow? All these questions were swirling around in her mind as the cab driver stared.

"You don't have my twenty-five bucks, Lady?" he asked, angrily.

"I thought I did." Tears came to her eyes as she fumbled around through the contents of her purse: a few containers of make-up, a mirror and an eye glass case which was empty. "And I can't go to my mom's. I just can't let her see me like this."

The driver turned halfway around. When he saw her shoulders which were covered in bruises, his frown suddenly dropped and he said, "Get me next time."

Suddenly, Catherine opened the door, her eyes full of tears. "I need to buy an outfit tomorrow for work and find a motel room. It doesn't matter now!"

The cab driver pulled out a card. "Here's a name of the local homeless shelter. It's just a cot in a big open room. For a night until your payday it might work."

"Thank you," she said.

From out of her side pouch of her purse, Catherine felt her change purse. "Wait!" She cried out in joy. "Lucky didn't know I had this!" She yanked out a small container which was beaded and shaped like a turtle. She pulled out a debit card and three twenty-dollar bills.

"Don't worry," the driver said. "Keep the cash; go buy yourself a nice dress for work."

Tears filled Catherine's eyes. "Thank you," she said.

"God bless," he said, restarting the engine.

Catherine jumped out of the car and hurried into the store. Shoeless and wearing nothing but a towel and bathing suit, she did her best to avoid those staring at her.

A store clerk approached. When Catherine turned and she saw the bruises, the woman immediately stepped back. "Do you need a doctor? Are you okay?"

"I have sixty dollars and I need a dress for the job I start tomorrow."

"What size do you wear?" she quickly inquired.

"I'm a 20," Catherine announced, glancing behind her. "Are any of your dresses on clearance?"

A man wearing a tag of "Store Manager" came to aid the salesclerk. "Our clearance items are on this rack. We might not have one for that price even with a discount." Seeing her bruises, he added, "I'll check though. You said you were a size 20?"

"She'd be on the plus side." The salesclerk immediately pointed to the rack to their right. "Try the red and black suit ensemble, Martha. I just had Beatrice hang a bunch in Plus. There should be a 20 or 22 left," the manager stated. "We also have shoes that just went on sale for $9.99. They were $29.99 but they are last year's style with the small one-inch heel."

"Short heels are my thing." Catherine sounded pleased.

From behind the rack of clothes, the salesclerk, Martha, held up two red and black suits. The pants were black, and the top was bright red with a V-shaped black neckline. The top appeared to be cotton, nylon mixture. It had been marked down from $55.00 to $24.99.

"What size shoe do you wear?" the clerk Martha asked.

"Six."

"There's a black pair on the top shelf. That pair has a slight defect. I may be able to sell it even at a better price," the manager informed the clerk.

Martha smiled. "Yes, Alex."

"While Martha gets you a pair of shoes, feel free to try on the clothes. The dressing rooms are over there." The Manager pointed Catherine to the back wall.

Catherine hurried to examine the outfit. She rushed back into one room with a curtain and slipped on the one size 22. It was slightly large in the hips. She decided the 20 would be too tight if she were sitting behind a desk most of the day. She left the dressing room and handed the manager back the size 20. "That one fits perfectly!"

The store manager handed her a box of shoes. Without socks, Catherine tossed one down to the floor and tried the right one on. The short, heeled shoe fit perfectly. She even liked the style and didn't care that they were last year's style. Quickly, Catherine tried the other side. The left shoe matched in comfort and Catherine picked the pair off the floor. "I'll take them."

"Follow me." The manager walked Catherine to the register. There were three other women in line and they gave her looks of pure disgust looking at her black and blue body in a bathing suit. Catherine held her head high as she waited.

He rung up the shoes for $4.99 and the entire cost was barely over $30.00. Catherine felt grateful. Somehow this seemed okay. She had no place to go, but she had an outfit for work tomorrow which was only a few blocks from here. In her purse, she had make-up. She might not have a place to sleep, but at least she would make her first day at work.

"You are very kind," Catherine said, thanking the manager, and she headed outside to figure out where she would go next.

Will was standing near the parking lot as she exited. When he saw her, he immediately strolled over and greeted, "Hi, Catherine." He glanced down at a sales receipt. "It's good to see you again."

"Aren't you Dr. Newport's friend that I met at The Spin Bottle club last weekend?" Catherine inquired. "Will?"

He nodded yes.

"Do you know where this store is? My sister bought this stupid thing." He pulled out a small garment bag from behind his back. "She wants me to return it for her."

"You're standing right in front of it. See the SF on the corner. It stands for Shannon's Fashion house."

Will showed Catherine the tag. "Can you believe she spent eight hundred dollars for a few strings?" It was black and silk with string ties over one shoulder.

"First of all, that's a designer bathing suit, not a dress, and for eight hundred dollars that is actually a SF bargain," Catherine said.

"Oh." Will grunted, rolling his big hazel eyes.

"You don't shop much with your sister, do you?" Catherine said, embarrassed she was standing in front of such a handsome man in a towel and swimsuit.

"I don't like shopping, let alone for my sister," he said sincerely. Catherine could barely look him in the eyes.

"Are you okay?" he softly inquired, gazing at her injured shoulders.

"Yes," Catherine announced, honestly frightened.

"Your boyfriend put those bruises on you?"

She avoided the question. "I start tomorrow at Castle Builders of the Great States. It's a great paying job so as long as I can do it, I'll be fine."

"You're not going back to Lucky, right? Where are you staying then?"

Catherine showed him the card of the Homeless Shelter the cab driver had handed her. "Could you give me a ride? I'm just going to stay there for a little while until my bruises heal. Then I'll talk to my mother about living with her."

Will gasped. "Stay here for a minute. You promise?"

"Promise," she said.

Will hurried inside and returned a few minutes later without the bagged item. He handed Catherine the eight hundred dollars. "My sister isn't coming back from Orlando for a month or two. You can pay me back when you can." He opened his wallet and jotted down a phone number. "Call my cell phone when you have it."

"You trust me?" Catherine gasped.

"Castle Builders of the Great States is the company that built my new office building. They are in the process of developing the Lansing Project which is a huge condo complex overlooking the river. I pre-purchased two for resale and will make a bundle next month. These eight hundred dollars can help you now."

Catherine couldn't believe it. "But I hardly know you."

"You're a friend of Jay's," he reminded her.

"So?"

Will proudly informed her, "He's a good man."

"Yes, Dr. Newport is."

"Jay's done a lot for me over the years, including being my sister's doctor and doing so much for my cousin."

"I don't know what to say." She fought back her tears.

"You don't need to say anything." Will pointed to a motel across the street. "Tell the woman behind the desk I sent you. The rooms are not fancy, but it will give you a private bed and your own bath."

"Are you seriously trying to find me a place to crash?"

"It's not much. Believe me."

"It's enough!" Catherine shook with emotion "I don't know how to thank you."

Will smiled, walking away. Catherine watched him strolling around the corner of Sharron's Fashion House. He disappeared in the parking lot among the many SUVs. Slowly, she pivoted and headed toward the dingy, small motel with broken windows and bars on the doors.

As she was opening the front door, a rat scurried past her feet. "Temporary," she told herself.

With her first paycheck, she'd be able to pay Will back. With interest.

CHAPTER 28

Jay wasn't expecting Will as he opened the etched glass door to his two-story mansion on Rock River Drive. "Will," he greeted. "Did you follow Catherine from the hospital?"

"She still hasn't called her mother. She went to the mall and bought some clothes for tomorrow. She was still in her bathing suit. Everyone was staring at her like she was some freak in the circus," Will snipped. "It was horrible. I was worried she might go back to Lucky's house, so I lent her some money by returning a piece of clothing from my sister."

"Which sister?" the doctor questioned.

"Neither one. I purchased the item when Catherine was in the dressing room. It was eight hundred bucks."

"Bill me."

"You're billed. Fred's outside her motel room now, across from the mall. I pulled him off of watching Lucky for a while so I could come talk to you. I'm not sure if Lucky got a good look at who saved Catherine, but the moment I took off he headed back to Key West to a meeting with Miller. He drove there, stopping by an address that rang a few bells."

"Now what?"

"Do you remember that murder case I did last year when the guy knifed his ex-wife and his eighteen-year-old girlfriend? That's the house and the cops couldn't pin it on him because of evidence handling problems. I'm having Fred check to see if he still lives there."

"So, Lucky may be connected to a murderer and not just drug dealers."

"If drugs are your line of work…" Will shrugged. "…they sometimes go in hand-in-hand. Needless to say, I'm leaving my black truck stationed at the office and am driving Fred's SUV now. I loaded it with the state-of-the-art surveillance because I don't want Lucky or even Catherine linking the black pickup back to me."

"How's Catherine's mental state?" the doctor inquired.

"For someone who just realized they're homeless and worried about their own personal safety, I'd say she's doing pretty well. She is looking forward to work tomorrow."

"You got anyone inside Castle Builders of the Great States?"

"Who don't we have inside?" Will smiled. "Catherine's safe. I even planted that they are building my new office building so I could even go in myself to check on her if anything comes up."

"That's a new approach." The doctor raised a brow. "You don't usually even speak to your clients, but today you offered her money and now you set it up so you can see her later."

Will admitted, "I'm breaking the rules. Sorry."

Jay walked into the kitchen and poured himself a glass of wine. He offered Will a glass.

Will raised a hand to decline. "Still on your clock, remember?"

"Things aren't as bad as they seem." The doctor took a gulp. "Catherine's employed. She's got a place to live, and Lucky is currently out of town."

"I don't like all this manipulation," Will admitted.

"I used to have a problem with that myself. Then I concluded my manipulations are temporary. It's simply necessary to get her out of a permanent and potentially fatal situation." The doctor finished his wine. "Without us what might happen to Catherine? Lucky is controlling, vindictive and a sociopath. We got Catherine away from him and now she has a chance for a real future."

"She's not going to get over feelings for Lucky right away," Will reminded him.

"Of course, that's a normal reaction. She might at one point even consider going back to him," Jay submitted. "That happened with Jennifer Martina. We had to lure her away with a third-party interest."

"Let me guess, if we need a third party interest with this one, it will be you."

"Don't be an idiot." The doctor smiled. He turned for a moment, heading toward a giant sofa underneath a large plasma television that was hanging on the wall. He plopped down and filled another glass of wine. "Although, I do see in Catherine a certain kind of beauty."

"I know what you mean. Hubba Hubba!"

That got the Doctor's attention. He sat up, placing his wine goblet on the glass coffee table in front of him. "Why all of a sudden are you starting to see things my way?"

"You should have seen those women in that store looking down at her. Sure Catherine's overweight, but she had the strength to ignore their insulting stares. She didn't give those women buying all those bags of clothes even an ounce of satisfaction."

"That's because Catherine's as good as they are."

"At the lowest point of her life, she completed her mission, to get an outfit for work. Not even the manager stopped her. He helped."

"How'd she look in the bathing suit?"

"No different than me in a Speedo." Will chuckled, patting his thick belly.

"So, you finally admit you have a weight problem! That's an improvement," the doctor praised. "You haven't lifted weights in a few months, have you?"

"Catherine may be overweight like me." Will grinned. "It still took everything in me not to invite her back to my house and tell her to start living with me."

"You're feeling sorry for her." The doctor understood. "We've done this before… just don't fall."

"I didn't say I was." Will rejected the idea. "I just find her inner strength very cool."

"She doesn't fool me. Catherine's frightened." Jay shook his head in disagreement. "No one could be in that position and not be scared half out of their mind. It's a good thing she has us behind her."

"Is it? I'm not so sure."

"Aren't you still interested in that stewardess Kat? She seemed quite taken with your charm," the doctor reminded him. "Maybe a few dates will keep you focused."

"I'm sick of short-term relationships with women who only want short term."

"You! Really?" The doctor chuckled.

"How many women hit on you on a daily basis?"

"I'm so wanted women practically throw themselves at me. It's not easy being such an attractive doctor, you know," he said sarcastically.

Will grabbed a pillow and smacked Jay in the head. "I'll let you know if my dating status changes."

"Remember, I'm the boss, and Catherine is nothing more than your client."

"I'm very aware of that fact. I've been eating, sleeping and drinking nothing but her tail for the last week." Will yawned.

"Keep things professional."

"Yes, Sir." Will opened the front door to let himself out.

"I find it odd…" the doctor grabbed the remote of the plasma television "…that we keep reminding each other of that."

CHAPTER 29

Jay entered his second story bathroom while removing his blue shirt and white silk tie. He unzipped his dark pants and lowered them and his boxer briefs to the Spanish tile floor. Naked, he raised the large blinds alongside his giant Jacuzzi bathtub. The moon's reflective light shone brightly through the giant plate glass window that overlooked the calm river below. His incredible masculine frame leaned against the window. From the second story bath, the view was exquisite. He stared out for a moment and then leaned over to run the warm water.

When the wet liquid reached the jets, he stepped into the tub and lowered himself gently into the hot, steamy bath. Uncurling, he leaned his sandy, blond-gray hair against the back of the tub.

He should be relaxing, he thought. But his mind drifted back to Catherine. "When is her next appointment?" He wanted to remember. It wasn't like him to know the appointments of all his patients, but he knew hers was only a few days away.

He'd be able to discover if she liked her new job. It was a good one from what he had learned, benefits and a good starting salary with even paid vacation time. This was an opportunity he had first learned about from Janet a long time ago.

His mind flashed back to ten years ago: standing over Janet, his patient in the hospital room; her face was covered in bruises. Her eyes were swollen shut; she could barely speak to him when she spattered out blood, saying, "You were right, Doctor. I should have left him. Please forgive me."

Tears stung his eyes but he quickly wiped them away. From the side of the tub, he grabbed a set of matches and lit four tall pillar candles. He grabbed the remote from underneath a thick white towel and flipped on the radio which was playing a tropical song.

"Jimmy Buffet," huffed a voice, "nice."

Horrified, the doctor realized an intruder was lurking inside his house. He sat up, watching the shadow of a large man creeping across the bathroom. He reached for his white towel. "Will, is that you?"

"Not the private investigator," the masculine voice replied, curtly.

The doctor's breath caught in his throat. He wanted to run into the bedroom for his handgun, but to do so would mean whoever it was would see him streaking across the floor. There was no telling where this man was in the bedroom and if he had a weapon of his own.

"Don't bother getting up," the voice ordered.

"Who are you? What do you want from me?"

"The real question is do I trust you enough to tell?" asked the stranger.

As long as he didn't see the trespasser's face, he would be kept alive, the doctor guessed. Instead of giving into the fear, he took a long deep breath and leaned his head against the tub wall. "Why have you come into my house uninvited?"

Noises coming from the bedroom indicated the shuffling of drawers. Something crashed and the doctor grumbled, "That wasn't my mother's antique vase, was it? It was imported from China."

"I've always wanted to go to the orient," informed the voice. "I've been twice to the Gulf and Korea."

"A military man?"

"Special forces unit," he gracefully informed.

"They certainly taught you how to break into places. You didn't set off my alarm."

"I'm really the best at sharp shooting." His shadow moved to where the doctor could see his enormous size, his trench coat and baseball cap.

"Are you here to extinguish me?" the doctor asked bluntly.

"You'd be too easy."

"Would it make a difference to you that I don't want to die?"

Suddenly the man took a step into the bathroom. The Doctor didn't dare look up at his face, but he saw his boot laced halfway up his calf of his black pants. A black gloved hand patted the doctor's gray hair. "In my line of work, you learn many deserve to die but don't wish to, Doctor Newport."

"So, you know my name. I find just the opposite in my line of work. My patients are trying to avoid suicide."

"Opposite sides," he said.

"What is it you want?" the doctor questioned again. "Money?"

"Not everyone can be bought. Although in this particular situation I was paid to gain information about one of your patients."

"I can't talk about anything that happens in my office."

"You should be questioning if you'll even see daylight again if you don't give me the information I need."

A clear death threat? Slowly, the doctor sat up and the man backed out of the bathroom. "Can I get dressed?"

"Stay in the tub."

"I refuse to give out patient information!"

"You already have," he said. "An associate of mine hacked into your computer system and obtained your files and emails for over the last three months."

"Then what possibly could you want from me!" The shadow pulled out a long gun and the doctor had to take a few more deep breaths before he questioned the intruder again. "What do you want from me?"

"Where is Lucky?"

"He isn't my patient," the doctor said.

"Where is Catherine Walters?"

"If you got my files then you know all about her."

"Victim of physical abuse. Yes, I know what she claims," the voice said.

"That is what happened. What is this about?"

From behind the wall came the gloved hand again but this time it dangled open and in the black wallet revealed a shield, that of a police detective. "I'm an undercover agent. We've been infiltrating the Millers in Key West for the past six months. Lucky is about to walk into a drug deal that's gone very bad. We need to make sure that Catherine is nowhere near Key West when we arrest him. She left the hospital in a cab and the cab driver refused to tell me where she was. He said Catherine had bruises all over her and that for all he knew I could be the one who did it to her."

"I see," the doctor said.

"So where is Catherine Walters?"

The doctor stood up and wrapped his muscular body in the towel. He stared at the man in the face. He was younger than he but not by much. A scar was across his left cheek and around his neck was a tattoo of an Indian Chief with a Bald Eagle on his shoulder.

"How do I know you're a real detective and not one of Miller's or Lucky's cohorts?"

"Either you give me the information I need or you'll be arrested. No offense, Doctor, but you don't look like a man who would last long in jail with such a pretty face."

"I want Lucky behind bars too," the doctor informed him. "He tried to kill my patient!"

"With a little help from you, we'll nail him."

The doctor smiled. "I'll show you where Catherine is as long as she remains safe."

"Then we have a deal."

"I'll take you to her."

The man nodded his head yes. The doctor took a look at his bedroom. Not in shambles, there was clear glass all over the floor where the entrance to the bathroom was. He glanced over to the golden vase with etched goldfish around the rim, his family heirloom still in one piece.

"Breaking the glass made me sure you wouldn't get to the gun loaded in the top drawer next to your bed."

"You know about that?" The doctor sounded amazed.

From behind his back, the man pulled out the doctor's weapon. "I'll be holding this for now."

"Whatever you prefer." The Doctor began to dress himself and the man turned his back not to watch. With the man's attention elsewhere, the doctor grabbed the cell phone off of his dresser, opened it, hit a few numbers and then closed it right before the intruder saw him stuff it into his pants pocket. "I hate violence. I simply have the gun for protection. It's licensed with the state."

"I haven't all night to worry about that or wait for you to get all gussied up."

"Shall we take my convertible?" the doctor questioned.

"I don't think so." He gave the doctor a quick shove forward. "Now move it."

CHAPTER 30

In a 1974 Nova, painted red with white flames, the doctor sat beside the undercover police detective. He got a better look at the Indian tattoo on the stranger's neck. Without his jacket, another tattoo of a massive spider web could be seen wrapped around his forearm. An oversized Black Widow spider was dangling in black and red perfect detailed ink on his hand.

"You like spiders?"

"I once dated this singer in an all-female band called Black Widow."

"She sounds like a Princess." The doctor smiled. "Did she have a matching tattoo made for you?"

The man laughed. "She had a spider tat on her arm."

"Shouldn't I at least know your name," the doctor said. "You obviously already know who I am."

"You don't need to know."

"How long were you in the military?" the doctor wondered aloud.

"I've seen more war and bloodshed than I wanted to." The man took a pack of cigarettes out of his pocket and lit one.

"Any problems with repressed memories?" The doctor rolled down the window and the breeze whipped in. "Military men with your type of war experience can develop post-traumatic stress disorders. Nightmares, some depression and panic attacks can occur years later."

He didn't respond.

"I'm sorry. I'm just trying to hold a conversation. It's not everyday someone breaks into my house," the doctor added. "You're going rather fast. The speed limit is 45 on this road."

"That's because we're being tailed. Do you know anyone who drives a green SUV?" the detective questioned.

The doctor turned around and noticed the SUV following two cars behind. He couldn't see who was driving. The officer changed lanes and the SUV followed; now they were only one small sedan apart. "No."

"You're sure you don't know who is driving?"

"I can't see the face," the doctor admitted.

He checked to make sure the doctor was wearing his seat belt. "Hold on, Doc. This is going to be a funky ride."

The car sped onto the interstate and quickly accelerated to nearly one hundred miles an hour as they raced in between cars and eighteen-wheel trucks. The detective drove underneath the bridge only to have the SUV do the same thing. "Hang on!" the detective yelled as they almost tipped on two wheels.

The doctor grabbed the door grip, trying to keep from sliding side to side in the seat. As they moved the two vehicles did a three-sixty. They got on the other side of the interstate heading back in the direction they had just come.

"It could be one of Miller's gang."

With the two vehicles this close the doctor could see who was driving. It was Will and he had a very angry look on his face. "Stop driving like a madman!" the doctor roared. "I know—"

He was cut off. "Keep your head down!"

The car rushed off the interstate exit again, this time heading straight into a large warehouse with the sign "LUMBER" written on the side. The detective spun the car around, opened the door and got out, holding his gun.

"Get down!" he ordered the doctor.

"It's not who you think," the doctor roared.

"Get down below the window!"

"No, it's not…" The doctor felt a hand yank on his shirt, and he was laid out flat on the bench seat of the car. He glanced up just as the SUV stopped right in front of the car. Will jumped out, with his own handgun and stood behind the safety of the SUV's open door. "Drop your weapon!" he shouted.

"Drop yours," the undercover detective returned.

"Will!" the doctor cried out. "He's an undercover cop!" Will immediately lowered his weapon.

The detective showed his badge and sheathed his weapon back in its holster. "You're Will Cilva, right? The private investigator with his paws all over my case."

Rushing to the doctor's side, Will ignored the detective and helped his friend out of the car. "You okay? I got your cell phone signal."

"Where have you been?"

"I got here as soon as I could, Jay."

"I was taking a bath when this undercover dick broke into my house!"

Will smirked as he came around the car. "Did you enjoy seeing my friend naked?" he asked as he punched the detective in the nose. The man fell backwards on his butt, allowing Will to kick the gun out of his hand.

The detective immediately jumped up, raising his fists. In an instant he tried to clip Will on the jaw, but Will ducked and punched the detective in the stomach.

The detective dropped to his knees like a lead weight. Grasping his stomach, the detective coughed and held up a hand. "Enough!"

"Get in the truck, Jay."

"He's coming with me," the detective gasped. "The doctor is showing me where Catherine is! I have to get to her before the Millers or Lucky get arrested. We have to protect her from their associates."

"We've got Catherine covered," Will said.

"If you don't tell me where she is, I'll arrest you both for withholding evidence." The detective quickly coughed again, trying to catch his breath.

"There are right ways of doing things and then there are wrong ways. You practically kidnap this very important doctor in the middle of the night… and force him to tell you information that you should have gotten from me."

"I'm important?" Jay flashed Will a superior grin. "How wonderful for you to finally see me in my true light. It's about time, after all these years of ignoring my advice!"

"How do you stand this guy?" the detective asked Will.

"He's one of those pompous, sarcastic asses that grow on you," Will informed him, reaching his hand out to help the detective to stand. "At least he's not an ex-military officer who thinks he's too good to consult a private investigator."

"Name's Carl Hayden, and I already had to take out a search warrant for the doctor's house and risking my badge consorting with you all. I've watched enough of this case to know this one needs not only my help bit that of the DEA. Besides, it's not my fault you're a rent-a-cop." The disgruntled detective fingered his shirt just above the bottom of his spider web tattoo.

"Didn't it ever occur to you that I would have told you exactly where Catherine is and we could have delegated some sort of surveillance schedule?"

Hayden shrugged. "I don't have any choice but to go along with you both now, do I?"

"You better alert your sergeant, or I'll be the first one telling him about the little naked roundabout you had with Jay. The doctor can't be connected. Would you prefer my arranging some sort of meeting tomorrow while Catherine's at work or do you need to see her tonight?"

"Tonight," Hayden ordered. "She's employed now? Where?"

The doctor smiled. "You really have no idea what's going on with my patient."

Hayden said, "And you, Dr. Newport, should be glad I don't expose what kind of help you provide to abused women."

Will put his hand on Hayden's chest. "Stop threatening him! Jay will ride with me, and we'll show you where Catherine is temporarily staying." Will held out his hand for Hayden to shake. "I give you my word. We won't move her again, without you knowing."

Will shook his hand quickly and then turned to get behind the wheel of his car. The doctor followed Will back to the SUV.

"Don't worry about the network being exposed, Jay." Will glanced over to the doctor as he climbed into the passenger's seat. "Even Hayden knows my word is as good as gold."

CHAPTER 31

Will parked the SUV outside the tiny motel across from the mall. Hayden's vehicle trailed and stopped far away from the streetlight to remain hidden in the shadows. The Doctor and Will climbed out of the SUV.

Hayden was staring at the rundown building as they approached. "You put Catherine in this dump?"

"It's a few steps down from my mansion…" The doctor smiled. "…but at least she doesn't have to worry about her own safety."

A young man around twenty on a skateboard scooted over to them. His long blond hair flew back to his shoulders as he jumped off the board and kept one foot on it as he tied his hair back into a ponytail.

"Hi, Blake," greeted Will, and then he turned to Jay. "Blake? He's new?"

"Yes. Nice undercover outfit," the doctor complimented the young investigator.

Blake smiled and shrugged. "Makes for fewer clothing changes. This way, I can compete in Florida's Championship X Games and then go right to work on the street. Works for me."

The doctor grinned. "That it does. Congratulations by the way. I watched you win the gold on television."

Will and Hayden stepped up to Blake, and Hayden immediately showed him his badge. He waited until Blake nodded that he understood he was a detective.

"A cop working with us?" Blake questioned. "I thought that was a royal no-no, Will. Didn't you say something about the pokies always gettin' in the way of our investigations?"

Will awkwardly cleared his throat. "This is a bit different."

Hayden enlightened him. "I'm not here to arrest Catherine. I'm here to see that nothing happens to her when the FBI and my undercover team take down Lucky in a drug bust tonight."

"Cool." Blake nodded his understanding.

Will's elbow in Jay's ribs drew the doctor's attention so he could point to a slightly ajar window on the second floor. He didn't take his eyes off the woman's shadow in the lit room behind the cheap shade. "That's Catherine's room."

Slowly, the woman removed a dressing gown and then got into bed. The light immediately went out.

Will immediately glanced back at the Doctor. "She looks like she's in bed for the night. Maybe I'll go join her."

"Not funny," the Doctor snipped.

Will chuckled. "Okay, Hayden. She's right there." He pointed again at the window. "Anything else you need? Blake goes by about every ten minutes on his skateboard. I'll be parked right here and you're welcome to observe, with us if you'd like."

"Yeah, I'll even let you use my skateboard," Blake quipped.

Suddenly the muted buzz of a cell phone came from Hayden's car. Carl hurried to his car and pulled out the phone, answering the call. Hayden. Sure thing…no! "What's the plan then?" Hayden continued to converse without the others hearing what was going on. "That soon? All right. We'll have to make it work."

"What's that all about?" Will questioned the detective as soon as Hayden tossed his phone back into the car.

"The bust didn't go down. Lucky left his plane in Miami, got into a limousine and went straight to a motel. We were told that the Miller deal was happening tonight. I guess we got some bad leads."

"So, you broke into my house for nothing?" The Doctor raised his arms. "I have a full line-up of patients tomorrow. So, if one of you could run me home, I'd really like to get to bed."

"When do you see Catherine next?" Will asked.

"In a few days. Why?"

"Find out if she still has contact with any of Lucky's associates," Hayden said.

The doctor turned a cold eye on the detective. "I hope you're not thinking about using her as bait to set up another bust, because if you are you can damn well forget it. Tomorrow is Catherine's first day of work, and I don't want that disrupted. This job is important to her wellbeing.

"So is catching Lucky," Hayden argued. "Now, listen here…"

The light flickered on in Catherine's motel room.

The hourglass figure stood, but she picked up the room phone and put it to her ear. The four of them realized that's what had awakened her, and not their argument. They listened as Catherine's voice clearly was heard through the open window.

"How did you find me?" she asked.

"Lucky," Will gasped. He turned immediately, searching the street. Out of the corner of his eye, he saw a flicker of a cigarette in a car halfway down the street. "Is that one of your team?" Will asked Hayden.

"No. Yours?" Carl asked.

"Nope."

"Great. There goes my cover," Blake complained. "That's gotta be one of Lucky's homies," he guessed.

"Leave me alone!" Catherine cried, her voice shrill. "Do you hear me? Leave me alone or I'll call the police!" She slammed down the phone.

Will swore beneath his breath. "I hope I get a shot at that bastard before we take him out of circulation."

"So, what do we do now?" the doctor asked, just as the car down the street flicked on its lights and backed around the corner.

"Did you get a look at who was behind the wheel?" Hayden asked Will.

"No." Then Will turned to Jay. "It's best I get you home. Let's hope whoever that was in the car, he didn't recognize you."

"I'm not afraid," Jay said. Through Catherine's open window, he could hear her crying. He made a movement as if wanting to go inside to comfort her. But instead, he pivoted and went back to the SUV.

"He cares for her," Hayden observed.

"The good doctor cares for all his patients." Will moved past Hayden. "Stay here with Blake if you want. You have my cell number, right?"

"Unfortunately, my department does." Hayden sighed.

"I'm keeping an eye on Jay's place tonight. If Lucky connects this to the Janet Network protecting Catherine, the doctor may be in as much trouble as Catherine is."

Chapter 32

Jay waved farewell to Will as he reentered his riverside home. Tired, he tossed off his clothes and crawled into his lavish giant bed. He covered himself with a thin, white sheet, turned on the paddle ceiling fan and rolled onto his belly.

It was then he noticed the light on his answering machine flashing red on the side table. He turned over and hit the button marked PLAY.

"Doctor, this is your answering service. Patient Catherine Walters called, stating she needed to speak to you and that it was an emergency. We had your partner who is on duty at the hospital give her a call but she refused to speak to him. Her motel number is 555-9090, extension 201. We just wanted to inform you. If we can be of further assistance, please let us know. Goodbye."

The doctor immediately dialed Catherine's motel number. It rang twice before she answered.

"Dr. Newport?" she questioned, anxiously.

"Yes, Catherine. I was told you refused to speak to my partner at the hospital. Is something the matter?"

"I'm in danger," she said, obviously frightened. "Lucky called. He found me here. I don't know how but he did and there is this skateboarder who keeps running up and down my street."

The doctor grimaced. "This is a motel number my phone service had me call. Are you staying at a motel?"

"Yes, I'm paid for a week, but Lucky knows I'm here."

"Do you still have the valium I prescribed?" he asked.

"Yes, Doctor." She sniffled.

"Take one and try to rest. At that low a dosage you can take up to three and you'll be just fine. It should gently aid you to sleep. If that doesn't work, I can prescribe a few sleeping pills."

"I've never been so scared in all my life," she whimpered.

His head leaned back against the banister on his bed. "I know you are, Catherine, but you can handle this."

"I'm not sure!"

"You've been through the worst of it now. You've left him. It may take a while for Lucky to get used to the idea of you not being in his life. He will get the point eventually."

"What if he doesn't?"

"He doesn't have a choice," the doctor reminded her, "unless you change your mind."

"No," she said firmly. "I never want to see him again, not after what happened in the pool."

"You're going to be okay."

"You completely understand me," she said. "It's been so long since anybody has really cared."

The doctor knew she was taking his kindness for more than what he was meaning it to be. "You're my patient," he reminded her. "Of course, I'm here for you."

"Can we meet tomorrow for lunch?"

Her question caught him off guard. Surprised and half flattered, it took him a moment to find the words. "I rarely eat lunch out of my office. I just don't have the chance between patients."

"I understand," she said, disappointedly.

He worried that he had hurt her feelings. "Don't take it personal."

She gasped. "There he is again. This guy on the skateboard keeps skating by the motel! Should I call the police?"

"No, I don't think that will be necessary. It's probably just a local kid out having a good time. Lock your door. If anyone tries to get in, then call downstairs and alert the manager."

"Okay," she agreed. "I'll take the medication and try to fall asleep."

"If you need me before your next appointment, drop by the office."

"I'm worried about starting this new job. All of this is going to affect how I work. I'm not that smart."

"Yes, you are. You are very intelligent, Catherine. You can accomplish anything you want."

She breathed. "It's wonderful having someone believe in me."

"Please get some rest. You've been through so much, but you're not alone in this. I support you 100% with this job and leaving Lucky. After seeing your bruises, there is no doubt in my mind that Lucky needs a lot of help and until he gets it you don't need him in your life."

"Good night, Dr. Newport," she said.

"Good night, Catherine. If anything else happens call me."

"You're on speed dial," she informed him.

He smiled, then said, "Sweet dreams." And then he hung up the phone.

He recovered the lower half of his muscular, tan torso with the thin sheet. Tossing his hands behind his head, he looked up at the ceiling fan for nearly fifteen minutes. Finally, when his eyes got too heavy to keep open, he closed them.

His mind drifted into a dream. He was on the dance floor dressed in a tuxedo. Suddenly Catherine—thin, with long raven hair that hung to her waist—strutted across the room in a long black and red gown.

He placed his right hand on the middle of her lower back. When the tango music began, he extended his left hand and grasped her right-hand fingers in a loose grip. She placed her left hand on his right shoulder, and he led her, walking forward, placing down his heel and then his toes. She mirrored his movements, landing her toes and then her heel. Twirling her, he was captivated by her gray eyes with every move across the floor.

Underneath the giant chandeliers, they melted into each other's arms, making a half-turn clockwise. Their bodies intertwined like lovers who had waited a lifetime to be in each other's arms. The music grew in tempo and so did the intensity of their entwined figures glide forward.

From his lapel, he pulled out a single red rose and Catherine clenched it in her mouth as the song ended. In one swift grasp, he tossed it to the floor. Slowly, he gently pressed his lips to hers for a kiss.

Beep. Beep. Beep.

The alarm woke him. The doctor sat up only to find himself covered in sweat and breathless as if he had really been dancing. He checked the phone and there were no messages either from his answering service or from Will.

The rest of the night must have gone well for Catherine. The doctor took a deep breath, relieved.

CHAPTER 33

After her first few hours of watching a training video, Catherine wasn't quite sure she was accomplishing all her tasks. Working the front desk, she greeted the employees signing in. Several times she answered the phone and jotted down messages for Dell Mitchum.

The phone rang again. She immediately picked it up. "Castle Builders of the Great States. This is Catherine, how can I help you this morning?"

"I miss you," came Lucky's voice.

Catherine froze. "Lucky! If you call here again, I'm going to call the police." She tried to sound convincing.

"You wouldn't do that."

"Lucky, I mean it! Stop calling me. I want nothing more to do with you."

His voice lightened. "What about all your things? I have your clothes and all the jewelry I bought you. Let me at least give them back."

"Keep all of it!"

Suddenly a hand came over the desk, took the phone from her fingers, and then slammed it down on the receiver. Shocked, Catherine glanced up and found Will standing in front of her desk. Her face revealed her surprise, and then a smile slowly crept across her face.

"Will?"

"Is Dell Mitchum upstairs yet?" Will asked. "I have the 11:30 Appointment."

"No, he's hasn't been in all morning," Catherine informed him.

"How nice to see you again." Will pointed down to the sheet, and with his index, showed Catherine that he had an appointment on her boss's list. "A few minor changes for my new office building."

"Why don't you have a seat? I'll tell Mr. Mitchum you're waiting the second he arrives."

Will moved over to the sofa near the front desk and picked up the newspaper. "The next time Lucky calls to harass you, hang up and call the police." He checked his watch, and then turned to the Sports page. "I'll even help you fill out the restraining order paperwork."

"Can I get you a cup of coffee?" she asked him. He nodded yes. "Black."

Catherine quickly went to the break room, poured Will a cup and hurried back to place it on the glass coffee table in front of him. He didn't seem to notice over the paper, so she alerted him she had brought his coffee by saying, "Black as spades, just as you like it."

She went back to behind the desk just as the phone rang again.

She tensed as she sat down, but answered as cheerfully as she could. "Castle Builders of the Great States. This is Catherine, how can I help you this morning?" She smiled when it turned out to be her boss. "Yes, Mr. Mitchum, you're first appointment, Will Cilva, is already here. Okay, I'll be sure to tell him."

Will picked up the cup of coffee and folded the newspaper. The second Catherine hung up, he asked, "Is he running late?"

"Actually, I have bad news."

"Not coming in, huh?" Will understood.

"He said something about meeting Janet Dunbar for lunch and for me to reschedule your appointment."

"These big wig types always have more on their plate than they can handle. I don't suppose he has anything available tomorrow morning?"

Catherine studied the appointment book. "It looks like the next time he's available is Friday morning at eleven."

"I'll take it," Will said. "So do you like working at Castle Builders so far?"

"I love it! Don't worry. I'm going to pay you back as soon as I can."

"I'm not concerned about the money. I'm more worried about that jerk who keeps calling you."

"That's really sweet of you to care." Catherine thanked him.

"What time do you get off for lunch?" he asked bluntly.

"I get an hour break in about three minutes." Catherine's eyes dropped from the giant clock above the entrance doors. "I'm not sure I should leave though. What if Lucky tries to grab me outside?"

Will left his coffee and closed the gap between them. "Let's go to the sub shop for lunch. It's on me. I've got over an hour before my next meeting. We've both got to eat, right?"

Catherine smiled. "Yes, I suppose that's true. I'll tack the cost of my lunch onto the money I owe you."

Catherine put the "out to lunch" sign up on her desk. Then she went around the desk to follow Will out the door. They walked several hundred feet to the restaurant on the corner.

There was a short line of five people in front of them when they got into line to place their order. Catherine's eyes were focused on the menu posted above. She couldn't decide between the cheese steak or meatball sub.

She glanced over to Will, and he was gazing down at her, grinning. She couldn't help but notice the way he was looking at her. He almost seemed interested in her.

"So, what are you hungry for?" she asked him.

"You'd slap my face if I was honest." Will winked.

Catherine chuckled. "I have enough men problems now."

Will nodded in agreement and then turned to tell the woman behind the counter, "I'll have a meatball sub and also whatever she wants."

"The same only half." Catherine liked his choice. "That will be thirteen dollars," the woman said.

Will opened his wallet, pulled out a twenty and handed her the money. She gave him his change and a card with the number 10 on it. He put his hand on Catherine's lower back to escort her to a table farthest from the counter. "This table should give us some privacy."

"This is nice." He pulled out her chair and she sat down.

"When was the last time you went to lunch with someone other than Lucky?"

"I can't even remember," Catherine replied.

He sat down himself and smiled across at her. "So how is the motel working out?"

"If you don't like it there, I know a few other places."

"There's only one problem. Lucky found me. He called last night. I don't know how he discovered where I was staying. It was awful. I even called Dr. Newport I was so scared."

"Jay?" Suddenly Will felt the wind whistling from his sails. "You called Jay last night?"

"You have no idea how much Dr. Newport's advice means to me. He always seems to know the right things to say to get me to calm down. He told me to take my medicine and be sure to call back if I need him."

"He said that did he?" Will tried to hide his jealousy with a smile. "That is just like Jay to play the hero."

"I don't know how I would have gotten through all this without him. He is the greatest."

"Yeah, Jay and I have been friends for quite some time. We've done a lot of stuff together."

"Is he married? I noticed he doesn't wear a ring."

"Why would you want to know?" Will questioned.

"Just curious. It's amazing a man who looks like that isn't married."

Will straightened in his chair. "You're not his type. I mean, I hope you're not wasting your time thinking about him in anything other than a professional manner."

Catherine's eyes tightened. "I'm sorry. Are you upset that I asked about the doctor?"

Will changed the subject. "How do you think Lucky knows where you are?"

Catherine heard the number 10 being called. "That's us. I'll go get our subs." She stood and hurried over to the counter. She picked up the plates and carried them over to their table.

"Thanks, Catherine." Will smiled.

"This place is fast." Catherine began to eat her sub. "I'm glad we get to have lunch together today."

"Me, too. I've learned a lot."

CHAPTER 34

Leaving Castle Builders of America, Catherine felt as if she was floating on air. It had been so long since she'd put in a day's work. She was tired, but on the way back to the motel she realized that her mother should know where she was staying.

Instead of making a right on Balley Avenue, she made a left heading towards her mother's house. She heard a motorcycle coming from behind and threw a quick glance over one shoulder.

It was the big Native American Catherine recognized from the day he'd approached her in the park. He didn't look at her as he passed on the street and stopped at the red light. A chill ran through her bones. There was something odd about that stranger. Of all people, why had he picked her to talk to that day? She still wondered who the Blake person was he'd mentioned. Maybe Blake was an old friend of his and he thought she looked familiar in connection with him. Still, it was unusual to think that she ran in the same circles as someone in a motorcycle gang.

On the back of his trench coat was the word "Justice" in black. Two axes with feathers hanging off them were in the center. It was obviously a custom-made coat. Whatever gang "Justice" was, Catherine hoped to never meet any more of them. When she turned the corner of the street, she discovered her mother back in the front yard, this time watering the pansies they had planted together. It was only a few days now, Catherine remembered, until her mother's surgery.

Seeing her, her mother immediately turned off the hose and started heading down the driveway. "Hi, Honey! I tried calling your house yesterday and no one answered. Did you get my message?"

"No, Mom. What's wrong?"

"Nothing. I just thought maybe we could go to dinner. Is Lucky out of town?"

Catherine shrugged. "I don't know."

Suddenly, her mother was staring at her shoulder. Catherine glanced down and noticed that the top of her bruise was showing. She immediately worried that others might have noticed it at work.

"What happened?"

"Before you freak out."

"Freak out!" her mother roared. "Did he lay his hands on you again? That bastard!"

"I left him," Catherine admitted.

Her mother smiled. "You did?"

"Yes, we broke up and now I'm staying at a little motel right outside the mall until I can save up for another apartment."

"Nonsense. You can live with me," her mother said. "I have the back bedroom and it will be perfect for you."

"I'll think about it," Catherine said.

"What's there to think about?" her mother inquired, her voice exploding out of her. "I want you to stay with me. Besides, I know how you can cook, and I wouldn't mind taking advantage of that."

Catherine laughed. "Oh, Mom."

"Hey, come on. I want you to stay with me. We lived together until you moved in with Lucky."

"Just not yet," Catherine said. Her mother's face showed her puzzlement. She didn't understand what the problem was, and her lips pursed in confusion.

"Maybe in a month or so."

"Don't you think it would be great if you are living here while I'm recovering from the operation?" her mother asked.

"No guilt, please," Catherine begged.

"I just don't get it." Her mother's voice lowered with disappointment. "I would absolutely love having you around. We could hit the outlets and shop away all our troubles for a while."

"Is that all you think about, shopping and chocolate?" Catherine inquired.

"What else is there?" Her mother laughed. "Of course, there are also men. However, I think we've both learned the hard way that they can sometimes be more trouble than they are worth."

"Mom, I think it would be best for right now that we live apart. Then when things settle, I'll move in."

Her mother reached out to her daughter and hugged her. "Whatever you want, then. My home is always open to you."

"Don't you think I'm too old to be living with you?"

"Are you kidding?" her mother pressed. "Why wouldn't I want to hang out with my best buddy all the time?"

Catherine grinned. "I love you, too."

"Now, tell me the real reason why you don't want to move in," her mother said, matter-of-factly.

"I'd rather not say."

Her mother took several steps back to the water hose and began to roll it back up onto the holder which was fastened to the side of the house. "I don't like this. You usually tell me things."

"All right." Catherine moaned. "I'm scared."

"You left him," her mother commended her. "The hard part is over. We can get a police escort when we go get your things."

"Lucky can keep everything he's ever bought me." Catherine grimaced. "The reason I'm not ready to move in yet is because I'm afraid Lucky might be dangerous for anyone I'm living with."

"You think he'll come after you."

"I know he will," Catherine said. "So, for right now, until he accepts that I'm not ever coming back, I think it's best that we live apart."

Her mother gasped. "I need you now more than ever. Besides, that jerk shouldn't be able to stop us from doing anything we want to do."

"Humor me, please."

"Absolutely not," her mother added. "Lucky has cost me enough time with you as it is!"

Catherine handed her mother a business card with the motel phone number on it. On the back, she wrote her room number. "You can always reach me here. If Lucky calls you or drops by, don't give him the room number."

"Don't worry. I'm calling the police if he ever drops by here."

Catherine smiled. "I just want you to be safe."

Her mother sighed. "I'm just glad he's in the past for you. There are so many other amazing men out there. Most are trouble, but every now and again, there's a keeper in the mix."

"You're right," Catherine agreed. "Ever since I've met Will Cilva and Dr. Newport, I've learned there are really great men out there."

"Handsome, too?" Her mother cocked her head inquiringly. "You have no idea."

CHAPTER 35

Night came and Catherine rolled over in bed, watching and listening to the sounds of a skateboarder below. Over and over, the young blond man went up and down the street at incredible speeds, jumping up and off the sidewalk.

Spying through the window, she waited until the skater stopped underneath a streetlight, checking the wheels of his skateboard carefully. "Hey," she called down.

The skater glanced up.

"Wait right there. I want to talk to you." He nodded okay. Catherine gathered up her courage, tossed on a cotton robe over her nightgown and hurried down the stairs. She went out into the sidewalk to talk to the stranger who had been keeping her up.

"How many times have you gone down this block?"

"Lady, chill."

"Chill?" Catherine tossed her hair back behind her shoulders as her hands clenched her hips. "It's one o'clock in the morning. I've been at work all day and the last thing I need to hear is skating all night."

"Sorry," he said.

Catherine snipped, "What's your obsession with skating right next to this motel? Who are you anyway?"

Someone approached from the alley behind Catherine, startling her. It was the huge biker with all the tattoos. He was wearing a baseball cap and trench coat. The moment she recognized him, she began backing away, her face growing pale. Why did this man keep showing up? Was he following her?

Hayden held out his hands. "I didn't mean to frighten you, Miss. I wanted to make sure he wasn't bothering you."

"Do you know Lucky?"

Hayden came forward, grabbing her by the arm. "Miss, I'm not trying to scare you. Please calm down."

"She's going psycho," Blake commented.

Hayden snipped at Blake saying, "If you wouldn't be so damn obvious skating so much up and down the street."

"I've got the Skating Finals next week. I have to practice."

Hayden tried to comfort Catherine with a pat on her back, but her body wouldn't stop trembling. "He's just a professional skater. Don't let him bother you."

"Do you both know Lucky?" Catherine's eyes darted frantically between them. "Tell Lucky I never want to see him again."

"Dude, she looks like she's about to pass out." Blake ran up the motel steps and grabbed one of the rocking chairs out front. He carried it over to her. "Here." He offered the seat.

Catherine did feel faint. She took a few slow, deep breaths to keep from hyperventilating. Her knees gave way and she sank into the chair. Hayden knelt down beside her and picked up her hand, gently rubbing the back of it.

Blake frowned. "We should tell her who we are, man. Before she needs to go to the hospital."

"No way," Hayden retorted.

"Do you want me to go to the SUV and get…you know who?"

Catherine jumped out of the chair, pushed Carl and shouted, "I'm calling the police. Whoever you two are…" she looked rapidly at one and then the other. "…the police can check you out!"

"Oh, no you don't." Hayden grabbed her before she'd taken two steps and pulled her back around. Across the street, the door of a green SUV opened, and Will jumped out.

"Let her go!" he shouted. "She's been man handled enough!" Hayden complied and backed away, his hands raised to show Will he was abiding by his wishes.

"Will, what's going on?" Catherine ran to meet him, her eyes wild with alarm as he caught her by the upper arms. She peered anxiously up at him. "Did Lucky hire these guys to keep an eye on me?"

Will shook his head no. "They're the good guys, honey."

"How do you know that?" Catherine's hands flew to her cheeks as she threw a horrified look at Hayden. After all, he looked a lot more dangerous than a kid on a skateboard. "Please, Will…" She looked back up at him, her eyes begging him. "Tell me what's going on. Why does this kid keep skating up and down my street? Who's the grimy biker? And why—"

"Grimy?" Carl growled. "I resent that."

Catherine ignored him. "Why are you here?" she asked Will. "Did Lucky hire you to watch me?"

"I can't tell you who hired me, but it wasn't Lucky," Will admitted. "Just know we're here to keep you safe."

"How do I know you're not Lucky's eyes and ears?"

"I'm your friend, Catherine." Will waved Hayden and Blake out of ear shot. Hayden got into a car parked in the alley, and Blake traveled just far enough to barely hear what was being said. He plunked down onto his board and continued to observe.

"You've got to trust me," Will pressed her. "We're here to protect you. Hayden is an undercover detective. Blake works for my Private Investigating firm, part time, when he's not a professional skateboarder."

"That tattooed giant is a cop?" Catherine gasped.

"Hayden is undercover working with the DEA and the FBI to arrest Lucky on drug trafficking charges. He's using Busi-Jet for Frank Miller."

"Frank Miller, the real estate developer," Catherine questioned, confused.

"Miller is a drug lord."

Catherine sat back down in the chair, shocked. "He seemed so nice."

Will went down on one knee in front of her. "Believe me," he implored her, his hands resting on the rocker's arms, "all three of us are here to protect you."

"So, you don't work for Lucky." She sounded convinced this time. "Who do you work for? Cops don't hire Private Investigators, do they?"

"I honestly can't tell you who hired me."

Catherine's eyes went directly to his. "Don't I have the right to know?"

"I must protect the identity of my employer."

Catherine wondered, "Does Dr. Newport know you were hired to protect me?"

"I wish I could answer that," Will said, "but I can't. "Now let's get you upstairs and to bed. You've had quite a day and you don't need any more stress." Will gave her his arm and Catherine took it. He slowly walked her up the stairs to her room.

"Get some sleep, Catherine," he said, turning to leave.

"You expect me to sleep now?"

"Try," Will said.

"Thank you," she murmured.

"For what?" Will questioned.

"It was one of you who shot at Lucky and saved my life in the pool, wasn't it?" Catherine questioned.

"I took you to the hospital in the back of my truck," Will admitted. "It was the scariest time of my life. I thought I had acted too late. Regardless of all this going on, Catherine, I really do care about you."

"I don't know how to thank you for saving my life." Catherine smiled.

"It's not necessary."

"You're quite good at what you do." She gazed up at him with tired eyes. "Aren't you?"

"I try."

"You really do want to help me, don't you?" Catherine realized.

"Yes, with all my heart."

"Lucky scares me to death now. How could he have been involved in all this drug stuff and I not know for so long? And the Millers? I would have never guessed that they were involved in a million years. They are all so friendly."

"I'll be downstairs all night making sure the real monsters get nowhere near you or this motel."

Catherine opened the door with her key. "Would you like to come in, Will? Maybe you would like a soda or a cup of coffee."

He nodded yes. "I wouldn't mind that at all."

CHAPTER 36

Catherine took in a deep breath as her key opened the door to her motel room. "Good, I'm glad you're coming inside."

Suddenly Will touched her arm and moved her to face him. Their eyes locked into one another's, hazel to gray-blue. Her breath caught in her throat; it had been so long since she saw desire in a man's eyes, other than Lucky's. Will was absolutely gorgeous. She could barely believe he seemed attracted to her, too.

Could this be happening? Catherine wondered. Did this incredible man want her as much as she desired him? Was that even possible? Her mind focused on her being overweight and bruised. How could he find her appealing?

"As much as I'd like to come in," Will admitted, "I just think I might not be able to control myself alone in a motel room with you."

"Excuse me?" Catherine whispered.

"You're just getting out of a very abusive relationship, and I don't want to take advantage of your vulnerability. I don't want to do that to you."

"So, you weren't just coming inside for coffee?" Catherine questioned.

"Believe me. If I went into this room with you, it would not be for coffee and it just wouldn't feel right."

"I see." Catherine's eyes lowered.

"Besides, I'm on my client's dime."

"I really don't want to be alone," Catherine said. "Not tonight. I still feel kind of shaky."

Will's frame tightened hearing her words. He took a step away and he balled his hand at his side to keep from touching her.

"You're a very beautiful woman, Catherine, and I'd like to be with you right now more than anything, but it just wouldn't be right. You need some time to heal from your relationship with Lucky. Just a few minutes ago you almost passed out you were so frightened, and you don't want to be with me any more than I want to be with you just because you're scared. If it ever happens, I want it to mean more than that."

Her face brightening, she smiled, and it actually looked like she understood. "I'll be okay."

"If I was to be honest, I'm not okay," Will admitted. "I had no idea that the police were watching you too and now I've got to go talk to Hayden who is not one of my favorite people."

"Why not?"

Will shook his head in disgust. "I used to be a police officer and Hayden was my partner. He caught me breaking into a few houses to find evidence on a murder case without search warrants. He told our sergeant, and I got kicked off the force, which is exactly what I deserved."

"It sounds more to me like over enthusiasm on your part than a lack of professionalism. Regardless, I'm so sorry."

"Actually, it worked out for me. I opened up the PI office and things have been good in that department. It's just Hayden won't ever let me live it down." Will pushed a hand through his dark hair. "He never wants me to forget that he was the reason I lost my badge."

"Don't let him get to you," Catherine advised.

"I try not to," Will said.

"Just ignores him."

"He's a hard man to ignore," Will reminded her. "At the time it happened I was devastated. Since I was a kid, all I'd ever wanted to be was a police officer. My father was a cop. Even my Uncle served. Hayden ruined my family reputation."

"That's terrible." Catherine's soft voice was conciliatory. "How did your father take it when you were kicked off the force?"

"Not well at all," Will admitted. "Most of my fellow officers understood. Many of them came up to me afterwards and admitted how many times they wish they could have done what I did to catch a killer, rapist or thief. They knew why I did it and didn't seem that upset about it," Will said. "Hayden is the one who came up to me afterwards and told me that following the law is what determines who a good guy is and who's a bad guy. After six months on the force, somehow I'd forgotten that for my own personal goals."

"He said that?"

"He was right." Will returned his attention to her eyes. "That's the moment I realized I wasn't cut out to be a cop after all."

"Do you still break laws to solve your cases?" Catherine wondered out loud.

"I'll do whatever is necessary to get the criminal and to save the lives of my clients. If that makes me a bad guy, then I guess it does. I learned the hard way cops have their hands tied."

"Do you think you'll ever go back to the force?"

Will sighed. "Being a private investigator is really what I am. It's a thrill for me to gather just the right information to solve a case."

"I can see you love what you do." Catherine noticed the spark in his eyes.

"I don't want to go back to the force. Not now."

"If it makes you feel any better, I'm glad you are the one watching out for me." Catherine smiled as she flattened her palm over his heart. "I know you're friends with Dr. Newport. He wouldn't be friends with you if you weren't a good person."

His slight smile bordered on a smirk. "Believe me, the good doctor's a whole other story regarding the law."

Catherine frowned. "What do you mean? Has Dr. Newport done something the police would be interested in?"

"It's not important."

"Yes, it is. If the doctor in some kind of trouble—"

"He's not," Will persisted.

"Are you sure?"

"Don't worry about it. Just forget I said anything, okay?" Will began to back away. "And thank you again for the invitation. It's just that if I walk through that door, I'm the bad guy all over again and that's the last thing I want to be in your eyes."

"Regardless, I don't think you'd hurt me."

"Still, you might have regrets," Will said, "and that possibility is enough for me to say good night right here."

"Perhaps another time…" Catherine smiled, "…you'll have some coffee."

Will kissed her cheek. "I just might." He smiled. "Good night, beautiful."

"Good night." Catherine opened her motel room door.

"Sweet dreams." He began to walk away.

"You, too," she whispered.

CHAPTER 37

Catherine had an appointment with Dr. Newport after work, so she wanted to visit her mother before going in to the office. Her mother usually went for her morning walk at seven so if she hurried, she could join her.

The brisk morning walk felt great. She glanced around to see if she could see Hayden or Blake following her, but she didn't see either one. She preferred it that way. If she were to be watched, they didn't need to be stuck to her like Velcro.

With the sun rising through the azure sky, Catherine enjoyed seeing the clouds float across the sky like big, puffy cotton balls. One cloud seemed to look just like a big lion about to pounce onto another cloud.

What an incredible day, she thought.

When she turned the corner, she discovered her mother already on her morning hike down the street and heading in the opposite direction. "Mom!" Catherine cried out so loudly, several pedestrians turned in front of her.

Her mother whirled around. The second she saw her, she changed gears and headed for her daughter. "Good morning, honey!"

"Hi, Mom."

"Isn't this nice? Aren't you working this morning?"

"Yes, and I have a visit in the afternoon with the doctor. So, I thought I would drop by and see you this morning."

"I'm glad you stopped by. I need the diversion. My operation is scheduled for Monday morning."

"Just a few days away now." Catherine forced a smile. "Is there anything I can do to help you?"

"Not really. I've eaten about a half a pound of chocolate. I've watched all my favorite movies to get my mind off things. I'm not exactly sure what else to do."

Catherine suddenly got an idea. She remembered the little white church where she had gone to pray and light a candle. A smile crept across her face as she recalled thanking God for Dr. Newport's help.

"Maybe you're looking for comfort in the wrong places. Maybe you've got a hole in your soul."

"A hole in my soul!" her mother parroted. "Now what are you babbling about? You're not making any sense. Believe me, I'll have enough holes and cuts in me come a few days from now."

"Not those kinds of holes, Mom." "Now look; you've tried chocolate, right?"

"I've gained three pounds this month."

"Keep walking and you'll lose it," Catherine assured her. "And you've tried watching your favorite movies, and that hasn't helped."

"So, what do you suggest I do? I've gone for long car rides and to the beach to watch the fishermen flex their muscular arms," her mother added. "That was fun. I saw a woman about my age catch a little sting ray."

Catherine inquired, "And how did that work out?"

"Fine. Until I got pinched on the toe by a ghost crab. I was standing right at the front of *its hole*."

"That must have hurt."

Her mother admitted with a slight smile, "It was small so not really."

Catherine gave her mother an arch smile. "Okay, what I mean by *holein the soul* is you haven't done any seeking comfort from a higher power."

Her mother suddenly stopped walking and faced her daughter. "You mean all those years of dragging you to Sunday school with your father actually paid off. You're kidding, right?"

"No, I think we should say a little prayer about your upcoming operation. I know it would make me feel better."

"You want to pray right here in the middle of the street?" her mother asked.

"Here, there, wherever. Wasn't it you who used to pray every time we got stuck in traffic?"

Her mother recalled the exact prayer. "God, make me a path and get us home."

"Exactly." Catherine gazed candidly at her mother. "When was the last time you prayed?"

For a moment her mother pondered. Then her head turned toward her daughter and she shrugged. "Not since your father left and never contacted us again."

"You haven't prayed in ten years?" Catherine gaped in surprise.

"I was a little upset about his leaving and then when Grandma died," her mother said, "I stopped going to church altogether."

"Don't you think it's about time you stopped blaming God for the things Dad did and say a prayer for help through this operation?"

"You think it will help?"

"I know it will." Catherine began strolling again. "Why don't you walk me to work, and we can stop by the church and see when Sunday services are? It wouldn't be bad if we started going to church on Sundays again together either."

"It's been so long since I went to church," her mother ruminated.

"I know it's been rough with losing Dad and then Grandma dying. I haven't been coming over as much since Lucky either."

Her mother's eyes filled with tears. "Don't say that! If it wasn't for you, I don't know if I could have made it through these past few years. You've been a rock of support for me, especially since I got the cancer diagnosis."

"Going to church together is one way we could spend some more quality time together."

"Sounds perfect," her mother said. "Maybe I should join the choir. Remember when I used to sing?"

"You have a beautiful voice, Mom. When you get strong enough, I think that would be a great thing for you."

"You're right." Tears slipped from her mother's eyes and rolled down her cheeks. "I've been trying to fill holes that just can't be filled without God. I just hope He hasn't forgotten about me after all these years."

"He doesn't forget anyone," Catherine reminded her. "I said a prayer not long ago for guidance to leave Lucky. I'm just trying to remember to keep Christ in my life."

"You're a precious daughter, Catherine." Her mother kissed her cheek.

"When I was six, I'll never forget when you looked me in the eye and said, 'All girls are Princesses when Jesus is King.'"

"Yes." Her mother smiled through her tears. "And what a Princess you have become!"

CHAPTER 38

Catherine sat down on the chair on the other side of Dr. Newport's desk. For whatever reason, she didn't feel like sitting on the sofa. She wanted to sit close while she asked him the questions that have been on her mind since last night.

When Dr. Newport entered, he briefly smiled at her and then sat down at the desk to thumb through her file. "Good morning, Catherine. Let's see, we talked on the phone the other night and you haven't called since. The sedative must have worked well for you."

"I'm not here to talk about my medicine," Catherine said coldly.

"Then what can I do for you today?"

"Let's discuss Will instead." Catherine leaned back in the chair and gazed directly into his eyes. Ignoring her attraction to the good doctor, she concentrated instead on conversing about more important matters.

"Will?" the doctor asked, confused.

"Your P.I. friend, the one you went on Busi-Jet to Miami with. We all happened to run into each other at the Spin Bottles Club."

"Oh, my friend, Will Cilva."

Catherine straightened. "Will took me to lunch yesterday. He saved my life from drowning in a pool last week. He made sure I got a motel room after lending me money. You know that guy. *The hero.*"

Dr. Newport smiled. "Now I see why the ladies take to him. He is a real knight in shiny armor."

"I asked Will last night to come in for coffee."

"You invited Will into your motel room?" The doctor's brow rose.

"Yes, he walked me upstairs to my door."

"And you invited him in?"

"Will is a very handsome man," Catherine reminded him. "He's tall, smart, and like you, very charming. He's even Italian, right?"

"I'm not sure of his nationality," the doctor admitted. "Don't you think you are rushing things a bit?"

"What do you mean, Doc?" Catherine smiled.

"You're getting out of a very long, difficult relationship, one with physical and verbal abuse. Although you have had some therapy to help you through a little of this, you still have a long way to go in building your self- esteem. Inviting a man into your motel room only a few days after breaking up with Lucky? Don't you see that there may be a bad pattern emerging of rushing into relationships?"

"Oh, it's a pattern now," Catherine said curtly.

"Now don't read too much into this. I mean, it is just my opinion. You could very well have real feelings for Will. He is a nice person from what I know of him, and he certainly is fun."

"Will is also a gentleman," Catherine informed him. "We had a late-night coffee and that's it. Of course, that happened after I was nearly assaulted by an undercover detective and Blake skateboarding back and forth half the night."

Dr. Newport placed her file on the desk.

"That's a very nice tie you're wearing, by the way."

"Thank you." He nervously smoothed his hand down the blue and gold patterned tie that matched his navy business suit.

Silence pervaded the room as they sat staring at one another for quite some time. It was as if he had much to say, Catherine thought, but not the courage to finally ask the questions to which he wanted answers. Finally, she spoke. "What's the matter, Dr. Newport? Cat got your tongue?"

"Catherine…" He paused.

"Yes, Doctor. You have something to say?"

He self-consciously cleared his throat. "What exactly did Will tell you about Hayden and Blake?"

"Hayden, is it? I didn't mention his name," Catherine said.

"I thought you did."

"Well, I didn't but you have indeed answered my next question. You knew that Lucky was being investigated for drug smuggling! Did you think I was involved in his illegal business too?"

Dr. Newport sighed. "No, I knew you weren't."

"Well, that's good to know at least."

"You're angry I kept this information from you," he surmised. "Do you wish for one of my partners to accept you as their patient?"

"You really think you can get rid of me that easily?" Catherine scoffed.

"I didn't say I wanted that outcome." The doctor lowered his tone. "In fact, it's been quite rewarding being your doctor. I've seen you come a long way and I'm proud of your progress."

"Even after I called your service in the middle of the night, half frightened by that skater?" Catherine twisted the sword a little deeper.

"I've probably gotten a bit too involved in your circumstances. As your doctor, I am to maintain a sense of distance."

"Really? Distance?" Her mouth tightened into an obstinate line.

"Catherine, I swear to you, I've given you proper care despite the difficult circumstances that have linked all these events together."

"That's the part that really gets me." With its emotional overtones, her voice caught in her throat. "These things that have happened to me are linked, but the police don't hire private investigators, Doc. Someone is paying Will!"

"Will has many friends in the police department. He's worked many cases that he needed their help to convict a perpetrator! Why do you even think he's being paid?"

"Will was hired to watch me. By doing so, he found out about Lucky's business ventures with the Millers and that's when that undercover detective must have gotten the DEA involved."

"That's a lot of guessing on your part."

"I even wondered if you might have been the one to hire him. No one but my mother knew of my problems with Lucky until after I came to you for help."

"So, you think I hired Will?"

"I just wish you would have told me the truth from the very beginning."

"And what is the truth?"

"That you started having feelings for me," Catherine explained. "That's why you hired Will to watch over me."

"Catherine." The Doctor rose from his chair, removed his glasses and placed them on his desk. He leaned across his desk, braced on his hands and stared directly into her gray eyes. "You're really reading more into this than there really is."

She rose. Her face merely inches away from him. "I believe you are the real knight in shining armor, Doc. I think you have feelings for me, and that is why you did all this to protect me."

Her lips moved in on his. He didn't move. Chemistry let her eyes drift almost shut and for a second their lips almost touched. Then suddenly, she looked into his eyes and realized he wasn't about to kiss her; she backed away. "Okay," she said.

"Okay, what?" he asked.

"You're not ready to kiss me yet."

"I'm never going to kiss you. You are my patient!" He came around the desk and placed his hands on her shoulders. "Catherine, you are in a very emotional state right now and I don't think this is the best time for us to be continuing with this conversation. You should go home, not before work, and then we'll talk further at your next appointment. Do you need a refill of your anxiety meds?"

"I am very attracted to you, Doc," Catherine confessed. "I probably shouldn't be your patient. I want to be honest with you about my feelings."

"The fact you are attracted to me isn't an issue."

"Isn't an issue?" Her mouth hung open. "What do you mean by that?"

"We'll discuss this at another time. Perhaps after you've had a little more time to deal with your feelings for Lucky and Will."

"Will?"

"Will does seem to be interested in you, and he's intelligent and responsible enough it appears to know it's not time for you yet to become involved in another relationship with a man. Perhaps when you are ready that is a way to go."

Catherine's eyes widened in surprise. "So, you really aren't interested in me? You'd rather I date Will?"

Out of frustration he stopped talking, hitched his butt on the edge of his desk and folded his arms across his chest. "All right, you will probably learn about this anyway and I don't want you worrying about who hired Will. I will admit to you that I did. I was concerned about your welfare."

"So, it *was* you?"

He nodded. "But I'm not paying him to tuck you into your motel bed at night. That's all on him."

"Jealous?" Catherine questioned him with a coy smile.

"Angry," the doctor admitted, rising to his feet. "He's paid quite well to watch. At the time I hired him I had no idea what Lucky was into or that the DEA and the FBI would find out how he was involved or who had hired him. I'm sorry that it's come down to this. If it makes you feel any better, Hayden broke into my home and saw me naked in my bathtub. It was quite embarrassing."

Suddenly Catherine's arms opened, and she embraced him. The doctor raised his hands to wrap around her waist, until finally he let go and backed away. "Why did you do that?"

"We're finally getting somewhere." Catherine grinned. "Are you telling me everything, Doc?"

CHAPTER 39

Catherine took in some deep breaths and lowered her gaze to the doctor's mouth. His teeth were clenched as if there was much more he wanted to say. She guessed there was more to the story and didn't want to back down until she got further answers. "What else isn't in my file?"

His eyes, haunted by inner turmoil, darted away from hers for a moment, as if he needed to formulate exactly what he was going to say. "I need your word," he said, his eyes returning to hers, "that what I'm telling you will not go beyond these four walls."

"You've already broken the law, haven't you?"

"I'm sure the background check and surveillance may seem like an invasion of your privacy." He stuffed her file in his top desk drawer. "It would not be approved of by my colleagues."

"So, you risked everything?"

"You, my Dear, are my greatest gamble. I normally don't take such chances but there is more at stake in your case. Your ex is dealing with some of Florida's biggest drug lords."

"So, Lucky will eventually be behind bars? Did you do that for me?"

"I did it for Janet."

"Janet?" Her eyes widened. "Why do I keep hearing that name? Everyone who has helped me has mentioned one Janet or another. Who is she?"

Suddenly the doctor's phone buzzed. He ignored it.

"You mean, who was Janet?" The doctor's eyes began to well.

The phone again buzzed, and this time a woman's voice came over the speaker phone. "Doctor, Will Cilva is on the phone. He says it's an emergency."

The doctor picked up the phone. "Will, what's wrong?"

"Put him on speaker," Catherine begged.

He pressed a button. "Will, Catherine and I are in session. I've got you on speaker phone."

"She knows?" was Will's first question.

"Yes, everything except who Janet was," the doctor advised.

"Blake is missing," Will blurted out. "He skated around your office building to keep an eye on your back entrance. There's no sign of him now."

"He's probably just skating around the block," Catherine said.

"Blake has a tracking device inside the heel of his right sneaker. Five minutes ago, he hit the panic button. It appears his position is traveling toward Busi-Jet. I have to get there before they can put Blake on a plane to God knows where. I'm sorry but I'm going to have to leave Catherine unprotected. I've called Hayden and let him know. He isn't returning my calls either."

Catherine suddenly jumped up and ran out the front door. The doctor called after him, "You have four patients waiting!" When he didn't respond she sat back down in her chair and smiled obligatorily at his waiting patients and shrugged. "I'm sure he'll be right back."

Outside, Catherine and the Doctor approached Will's green SUV parked at the curb. Will immediately lowered the dark window. "I called the police and left a message for Hayden," he said. "That's all I can do. "I'm going after Blake."

"Are you armed?" Jay asked.

Will pulled his jacket aside to show the doctor the Sig Sauer in his shoulder holster. "Would I go after them if I wasn't?"

"I'm going too." Catherine ran around to the passenger's side and jumped into the SUV.

The doctor's mouth tightened in a stubborn line. "No, you're not, Catherine! Leave this to Will and the police!"

She slammed the truck door and quickly buckled up. "It's Blake's life on the line here, all because of me. I'm going!"

"Actually, Catherine coming with me isn't a bad idea," Will told the doctor. "I'll park the truck far enough away from the airport to avoid being seen. And having her with me I'll at least be able to keep an eye on her."

"Absolutely not!" the doctor argued. "One of my partners isn't here today. Catherine can wait in her office and come home with me after my last patient."

"What about Blake?" A spasm of irritation crossed Catherine's face. "He's in danger and it's your fault!"

"My fault?" The doctor tossed up his hands.

"You're the one who hired Will's agency in the first place," Catherine retorted, angrily.

Margie stood in the office doorway, one hand on her hip, the other holding the glass door wide open. "Dr. Newport!" Her shrill voice carried across the street like fingernails on a chalkboard. "Should I cancel the rest of your afternoon appointments?"

The doctor screamed back, "Can't you see this is a crisis?"

The secretary gave him a startled, frightened look, along with one young boy who was peering out of the waiting room's large plate glass window.

The doctor huffed, mumbling, "Now I'm the one needing medication."

"Get in the truck, Doc!" Will roared. "I don't have time to argue, and I don't want Catherine in any more danger than she already is."

"Cancel the rest of my appointments today," the doctor shouted to Margie as he ran around to the passenger side of the truck. "I've got an emergency!"

"You need an emergency attitude adjustment!" Margie shouted back and then slammed the office door behind her.

He motioned Catherine to scoot over so he could jump in. Slamming the door, he sighed. "Remind me to give her a raise."

"You weren't very nice to her," Catherine said as she worked to fasten the middle seat belt around her. "You should watch your tone."

"Yes, mam." His mouth crimped in mock annoyance, and Catherine rolled her eyes. She barely got her seat belt fastened before Will took off, his hands gripped tightly around the steering wheel. The doctor was still buckling up when the truck skidded around the corner. Will pressed the accelerator down, and they sped down the street toward the small private airport where Lucky based Busi-Jet. "I shouldn't have raised my voice at Margie," the doctor agreed, "especially in front of my patients."

"You are human," Will reminded him, as he quickly darted through a small patch of grass to change streets and avoid the red light.

He slid a wary look at Catherine. "One of us obviously doesn't think so." He jerked on his still unfastened seat belt that was no longer letting him adjust it. "You should have trained your men better," he groused.

"Oh, will you stop?" Catherine reached for his seat belt, batting his hands away so she could lean across his lap to run the belt all the way back into its housing. She pulled it back out and promptly snapped it closed. "There. Now quit fussing."

"Fussing?" He glowered at her. "Children fuss, not grown men."

"Yes. And does that tell you anything?"

The doctor's stony expression turned bright red with exasperation. "I'll have you know I am not a child!"

"Oh, for Pete's sake!" Will bellowed. "Both of you are acting like children." He threw them an irritated look. "Just in case you've forgotten, Blake's life is hanging in the balance here!"

Catherine's brow crinkled in worry. "Do you think they've hurt him?"

"Blake is tough," Will assured her, "but if they've grabbed him, they took him down hard. That's why I'm so concerned."

Suddenly the truck slowed down and Will steered it into a giant grass field. When it reached a tall chain link fence, he pulled to a stop and turned the engine off.

"If you see any vehicle coming close to this truck, drive off and call the police. Tell them your location while you're hauling ass." He looked directly at Jay. "Do you get me? Don't stop for anything or anybody."

The doctor nodded. "No problem."

CHAPTER 40

Will climbed over the fence and ran toward the main building of Busi-Jet, about a half mile away. He had his gun cocked and ready to shoot at a second's notice.

In the truck, Jay and Catherine could see the building over the tall, yellow grass helping to conceal Will's approach.

"I'm sorry," Catherine apologized. "I just realized I wouldn't be alive now either. Will is the one who pulled me out of the pool. If you hadn't hired him, I would have been murdered that night. You saved my life too."

"Did I?" The doctor shook his head no. "Lucky was angry that you got a job and was leaving him. He was angry because I called in a few favors from some friends and got you a job."

"You got me my job?"

"Yes," the doctor admitted.

"Is there anything else I need to know?"

"You need to know about Janet."

"All right." Catherine positioned herself to sit facing him. "Who's Janet?"

"Janet was one of my first patients. She was in an abusive relationship, like you, except even worse. Not only was her husband verbally abusive and controlling, he would beat her on a daily basis for no reason. I asked her many times during our sessions to leave that son-of-a-bitch."

"You called him a son-of-a-bitch?" Catherine questioned.

"My exact words to Janet were something along the lines of, 'If this relationship seems troubling to you, there are other alternatives such as living with a relative or friend'."

Catherine smiled. "That seems much more like you."

"He had her so controlled she had no friends and her family wouldn't step in to help her because they were as frightened by his abuse as she was. I tried so hard." Suddenly his eyes welled with moisture. "I knew it was a losing battle, but I just didn't want to give up on her. She was smart and pretty. She loved pottery of all things. She made me this weird, shaped coffee mug."

"You liked her."

"Doctors aren't supposed to get personally attached to their patients." Tears started tracking down his jaw line. "But any doctor worth a grain of salt always does! It's wrong not to care when you're the one in charge of that person's wellbeing. Janet suffered. I saw every bruise, every senseless mark that ass put on her body."

"Were you in love with Janet?"

"It wasn't like that."

"It's not like that with me either, is it?" Catherine questioned.

The doctor wiped his tears. "I loved Janet. She was my patient and I cared for her as if she were my own sister. I saw her every week and didn't charge her any co-pays. I didn't even charge her insurance because I knew her husband would use it as another excuse to beat her up. And then one night, I got a call from my service telling me Janet was in the hospital and needed me immediately. I went of course."

He broke down. Catherine wrapped her arm around him and held him for a moment. "What happened?"

"She was black and blue and swollen from head to toe. I didn't even recognize her! I had to ask the nurse if that was really her! Then she spoke and I knew that horribly brutalized woman was Janet." He cried harder. "Her last words to me were an admission that I was right, she should have left him. She was in shock, and they couldn't get her stabilized. She died holding my hand."

"Did they arrest her husband?"

He nodded. "I testified at his trial. I made sure they knew how many bruises I saw but it wasn't enough. It couldn't bring that precious, sweet woman back to my office. For what he did, her husband is serving three life sentences."

"Justice prevails."

"That wasn't justice in my book. Not for the kind of treatment Janet suffered. Since then, I've helped dozens of women like Janet. Like you. These women are loyal to me; they know why I helped them and in return they help me help other women who are being abused."

"So that's what Janet means?" Catherine gasped.

"I eventually tell each of them who Janet was and why I do what I do. Not a single one of them has ever been angry at me for it… until you. Most of them have been quite thankful that I got them jobs and made sure they were safe until they were out of danger."

"You make it sound so simple, like it wasn't an invasion of my privacy."

The doctor wiped his eyes. "Every time I see this kind of abuse it makes me sick. So many women have come into my office, one after another, with bruises and broken bones. So many of them get into more bad relationships, repeating this very dangerous pattern of abuse."

"That's why you wanted me to wait a while before dating Will."

"Will is a bit of a hard ass, but he isn't abusive," the doctor explained. "And, frankly, I overstepped on that. You could do a lot worse than Will. He's helped me so much with these cases that I know he'd never beat on a woman. I'm not exactly sure why I got so angry."

"So, all these women who said their name Janet knew I was being abused and wanted to help me?"

"It's quite beautiful how the Janet Network operates behind the scenes."

"Is it?"

He looked directly at her. "Like I said, you're the only one who has ever complained that I hired Will to protect them! Most were thrilled someone was there for them."

"All these women fall in love with you, don't they? They see you as some knight in shining armor, ready to protect them. And then there's your good looks. How many of these women have fallen for you?"

"I don't know." He glanced over to her.

"Have you ever been with any of them?"

"No," he admitted, appearing somewhat offended she'd asked. "Some of them are still my patients."

"So, you break all the rules except that one," Catherine said, sarcastically. "How noble of you to remain a gentleman."

"There's a reason." The doctor watched Will, who'd reached the building. He crouched, peering around the corner of the building as if he might be listening to something. "You're right, Catherine. Blake being in danger is my fault, and I'm going to do something about it. I'm giving Will five minutes and then I'm going after him."

"That's not what he told you to do, Doc."

"Maybe not, but that's what I intend to do."

CHAPTER 41

Catherine watched the doctor head through the tall grass toward Will, who now stood next to the giant hanger door, which hung open on its tracks. His back to the building, he surreptitiously peered in through the opening.

The doc and Will were risking their lives and here she sat safely stowed away in the truck, gnawing anxiously on her upper lip. She was doing absolutely nothing to help either Blake or herself, and it wasn't sitting well with her. Not by a long shot.

In a rush of energy, Catherine burst out of the vehicle and climbed the fence to run after the doctor. Twice he motioned her to return to the truck, but she ignored him. When she reached the building the doctor stood shoulder-to-shoulder with Will. He looked resigned to her presence, but Will's eyes were seething. She could almost hear him grinding his teeth.

Trying to catch her breath, she disregarded him and put her back to the building alongside them. She showed them the best dogged expression she could come up with and told them, "I want to help."

"Lucky has a gun, Catherine," he growled under his breath. "Get back to the truck!"

"No." She spoke low, but with grave determination. "I'm here, and I'm staying."

"Judas Priest, the two of you are going to be the death of me yet."

"Knock it off, Will. We're here; live with it. What's going on in there anyway?" the doctor whispered.

"Blake and Hayden are tied up back-to-back in two chairs. Lucky's beaten them up pretty badly, but they're conscious and alive." Lucky was pacing in front of them, his balled fist covered in blood.

"I'll ask you again!" Lucky yelled. "How much does the shrink and this P.I. know?"

Blake spit out blood. "We don't know a thing!"

"Let the kid go," Hayden pleaded. "He won't let anyone know what happened here today!"

"Right, Pig!" Lucky said, his lips pinched with suppressed fury as he punched Hayden in the nose. Hard. Blood sprayed, but Hayden remained conscious and even managed to give Lucky a venomous glare.

"So why all this interest in Catherine? Why were both of you outside her motel room all week?" Lucky spit out the words, his voice starting to grow frenzied. He paced between questions, anxiously raking his clean hand through his hair. "Are the cops investigating my business too? Or just my personal life?"

Carl answered, "We're just friends! That's all! Catherine said she was leaving you."

"Who is she leaving me for? The doctor?" Lucky smirked. "He doesn't look like he could wipe his own nose.

"This is a complete misunderstanding, dude," Blake worked to gasp out. "We don't know nothin' about nothin'."

Lucky pulled his gun out of his waistband and pressed it to Blake's temple. "Then I guess I'm killing you both for nothin'."

Will cursed beneath his breath. "Lucky's got his gun pointed at Blake's head."

Will pulled his backup gun out of his boot. "I know you hate violence, Jay, but since you insist on being here, you might have to use this."

The doctor nodded.

"Stay here." Will pointed his finger at her, in the affirmative, and accepted the small thirty-eight. "Catherine..." Will's imploring eyes met hers, "...*please* go back to the truck," he begged her. "I put in a call to the police. They should be here any minute."

"Blake may not have a minute," she argued.

Suddenly a gun shot rang out inside the hanger, and Catherine screamed. Immediately, knowing what she'd done, she clapped both hands over her mouth. Her saucer eyes peered over her hands at Will. Then she dropped her hands, along with her shoulders. "I'm sorry." Their cover blown, Will and the doc ran into the shadowy interior of the hanger, guns aimed. Will heard Catherine's footsteps follow, but he didn't take his eyes off the small passenger jet that had started its engine run-up. Will aimed at the man just pulling up the stairs but couldn't get a shot off before the stairs melded into the fuselage and latched closed. With the whine of the twin engines nearly deafening, the plane headed right for them. Lucky was piloting. Both Hayden and Blake no longer sat in the chairs.

"They must have our people on the plane! Aim for Lucky!" Both guns spit fire at the cockpit, but the plane continued toward them, the bullets merely bouncing off the windshield, and ricocheting off the walls. The doctor kept shooting, until finally at the last moment, he jumped aside to avoid the plane. Will began to run after it, shooting.

"It's bulletproofed," Catherine yelled after him. In the distance, sirens began to sound.

"Now they come," the doctor sniped as he came to stand beside Catherine.

Will rushed back into the hanger and over behind the desk, where he grabbed the last set of keys on the hooks and headed towards the jet helicopter parked at the other end of the building.

"You've got to be kidding." The doctor grabbed Will's sleeve and tugged him to a stop. "What do you think you're doing? Let the cops handle it from here."

"We can't let Lucky take Blake and Hayden out of our sight, and I'm willing to bet there won't be anybody in those squad cars who can fly a Bell Ranger."

"And you can?"

"I can fly it," Will announced, and then spun to slap a palm-sized button beside the door. The angled roof began to whir open above the chopper.

The doc stared after him, his mouth gaping open in surprise. "C'mon, Doc. You can gather flys later."

Catherine grabbed him by the hand and towed him along behind her as she ran for the chopper. She shoved him into the front seat, and jumped into the back seat of the helicopter to buckle in. Will was already belted into the pilot's seat and the doctor was managing to do the same in the passenger seat.

"One of them might already be dead. I want you both to prepare yourselves for that," Will warned before turning the key to start the engine.

The blades began to turn with a whine, turning faster and faster until the familiar whomp-whomp of the blades blended with the high whine of the jet engine, making it impossible to hear each other talk. Will put his radio headset on and motioned for Jay and Catherine to do the same.

The helicopter lifted off and ascended straight up through the open roof. Once Will had it high enough to fly over the building, he immediately turned and followed after the small jet that was just now lifting off the end of the runway.

"We've got to get to them before they land anywhere near the Miller's property in Key West," Will said over the radio.

"Why? What's at the Miller's?" Catherine asked.

"Guns and more guns," Will explained. "Hayden told me all about the surveillance of that property. They use the Busi-jet planes to fly cocaine over the ocean. They put the coke packed in watertight containers surrounded by salt. Below there's a boat waiting and once the salt melts the airtight containers float to the surface so that the boatmen can transport the cocaine."

"How much cocaine?" the doctor wanted to know.

"Millions every month," Will told him. "That's why this place is under surveillance and is so very well protected. The salt packing is done right in the mansion. There is an airplane strip on the property, and planes fly in and out in the middle of the night so no one sees. They've gotten everything with night vision cameras. Lucky is their main pilot. The bigger the load, the more likely he is the one in charge."

Catherine gave a startled gasp. "I never knew any of this."

"The DEA knows that or you would have already been arrested," Will informed her. "Now we're caught in the middle of what the DEA and FBI should be handling."

"How did Lucky get his hands on Hayden?" Jay asked.

"I don't know," Will said, "but when he failed to report in at the station and then Blake went missing, I knew Lucky had done something with them."

"So, Lucky started suspecting the police were hanging around my motel for more than protecting me?"

"Probably," Will said.

"Well, we'll never catch them in this thing," Catherine groused. By now, the twin-engine jet was so far ahead of them they were no more than a shiny dot on the horizon.

"It looks like they're not flying a direct route to Key West," Will informed them. "But that doesn't mean we can't. Hang on."

CHAPTER 42

Catherine tightened her seat belt until she was sucking in her belly. Even so, when the helicopter took a sudden dip, she screamed bloody murder.

With the jet plane no longer in sight, Will kept checking his location finder for the remote tracer planted on Blake. The helicopter flew in between giant Washingtonia Palm trees and over enormous sand dunes. Flying so close in between the palms, the helicopter chopped off one of the large fronds and it came crashing down onto the beach. Startled by the falling limb, seagulls deserted the shoreline and flocked into the path of the helicopter.

Catherine's hands flew in front of her face as Will did his best to fly the helicopter out of the way of the bird barrage. She took a few deep breaths, gained the courage to peek, only to discover a pelican veering off the windshield by only a few feet.

"Let's not hit any mailmen," the doctor said. "I know how you like them."

"Not the mailmen." Will laughed.

"Remember when I sent you to cover Mildred and she turned out to be homeless and living under the pier? You just caught her pulling out one of those airbeds and a pelican flew over your head and…" The doctor started to chuckle loudly. "Sorry I didn't… well, I did have to pay for the dry cleaning."

"I had the cleaning lady call you to confirm it really happened." Will smiled back. "That was a crappy day."

"Literally," the doctor said and grinned. "We've had some interesting times, haven't we? It's been fun while it lasted."

"What do you mean? Your Janet Network is all good," Will reminded him. "This bust will only confirm that we are helping more than abused women. If this gets the Millers behind bars, we're getting millions of dollars of drugs off the street."

The doctor glanced back at Catherine who finally lowered her hands long enough to explain. "He means to reveal the truth of what he's been up to, the entire Janet Network will crumble."

Will gasped. "Why would you do that? This man is a hero! He's helped save hundreds of women, gave them a new start."

"He hires you and your men to invade people's privacy and then ignores the ethics of his profession," Catherine countered. "Look at what's happened to Blake and Hayden! We don't even know if they are even alive right now!"

The helicopter hovered over the waves closely, and then tracked up a giant dune; finally, it cleared the sand hill to pen a vista of mansions with enormous landscaped lawns. Among these tall structures and trees, the helicopter began to slow.

"We're close now," Will alerted them.

"I did what I felt was necessary to save life," the doctor said to her.

"With no remorse over all the laws you broke," Catherine reminded him. "Don't you understand that what you are doing has consequences, or are you so used to everyone covering your tracks that you've become as much of a hoodlum as these guys?"

"Don't you dare compare Jay to criminals like Lucky and the Millers!" Will shouted, then he turned to the doctor, saying, "She doesn't see the big picture here."

The Doctor huffed. "We've got to make sure Blake and Hayden are okay or Catherine's right. My actions led to this."

The helicopter descended onto the middle of a giant lawn. An elderly couple burst out of the three-story house onto their patio. The man was wearing multi-colored golf pants and the woman a sundress and pink sneakers. Hunched over, he started waving a fist and began yelling, but whatever he was saying was muted to them inside the chopper.

"The Millers live about two blocks from here." Will shut down the helicopter. "You guys ready?"

"I'm ready," Catherine said.

"Doc?" Will shot a glance over to him, but he was staring at Catherine.

"You should have told me that you had developed feelings for me," the doctor said to her. "I would have explained about transference."

"You were the one person I trusted! Do you have any idea how many lies you told me to hide the truth?"

"I merely maintain the Janet Network," the doctor reiterated. "Now we really should discuss this crush you have on me. You need to know my personal situation, so you won't take my lack of interest so personally."

"Did it ever occur to you that maybe my feelings are growing for Will, not you?"

"They have?" Will glanced over at Catherine. Their eyes met and he smiled at her. "We'll have to go out again sometime."

"I'd like that." Catherine gave him an animated smile.

"I hate to break up this love fest," the doctor said. "But we better get out of here before this couple sic's the family dog on us."

Will finally tore his attention from Catherine to watch the man dodder toward them. He shed his earphones and cracked his door open. The man raised his fist and shook it at Will. "Get off my lawn before I call the police!"

Will waited until the propellers stilled and then opened his door all the way. "Yes, sir, can you do that for us and tell them to go to the Miller's address. There is an undercover officer there who may have been shot."

"Shot?" The man gaped at Will. The elderly woman grabbed her big straw hat to keep the still revolving rotors from blowing it off. "We aren't in the mood for games! The Millers are fine neighbors."

"For drug Lords I suppose." Will reached in his jacket and pulled out his wallet. Making sure they saw his holstered gun, he then handed the man his Private Investigator's business card. "Tell them Detective Carl Hayden may have been shot and is being held against his will at the Miller residence. Do I have to make the call myself?"

"We'll call them," the woman quickly assured him.

"And stay indoors," the doctor advised them.

"We will." The man immediately grabbed his wide-eyed wife and steered her back inside the large house.

Will, Catherine and the doctor trotted through the yard and headed onto the street. There were hardly any cars on the road, but several kids on bicycles had stopped outside on the street, staring at the helicopter.

"Can we go for a ride?" one asked.

"Did the Jackson's buy that?" another wondered.

"How much does a helicopter cost?" the third young boy asked.

Catherine smiled at them and said, "You boys better get inside. Tell your parents to do the same."

Will held up his gun and the young men immediately took off on their bikes, heading down the street.

"Just so you know," the doctor said, "I did what I did because I liked you and saw your potential."

"Did it ever occur to you that my feelings might not be transference? Perhaps I see that in you, as well, even if we are only going to be friends." Catherine sighed.

"The real reason you are so upset right now isn't because you are angry at me. It's because you are scared. Instead of concentrating on the horrible danger you're in, disassociate and think about something else," the doctor suggested.

"Excuse me, Doc," Catherine snapped. "You seem to be analyzing me as I'm walking straight into gunfire! Shouldn't we be concentrating on the business at hand?"

"She's right, Jay. Look there." Will stopped and pointed to the twin engine turbo prop coming in for a landing well behind the stunning plantation house at the end of the dead-end street. They stood gazing at the enormous four-story mansion. It was festooned in majestic palms and ornate fountains. "It looks like the Miller's private landing strip is behind the house." Will checked Blake's tracer. "Blake appears to be in the separate garage, over there at the side of the house."

"Maybe we should wait for the police," Catherine suggested.

Will continued to study the tracer. "I don't think we can wait, Catherine. Blake is being moved to the back of the mansion right now."

"What do we do then?" she asked.

"I say we go in and do what we can to secure the property. If I don't miss my guess, they're either being moved via that prop job that just landed or a specialist has been brought in to torture the information out of Blake and Hayden that Lucky hasn't been able to get out of them."

"The Millers will want to know what we've discovered about the inside of their drug operations," the doctor provided. "They've got to be worried about losing millions. Hopefully, that's enough to keep Hayden and Blake alive a bit longer."

CHAPTER 43

Will grabbed Catherine by the arm and dragged her around behind a hedge, ducking slightly so their heads would not be seen. The doctor followed closely, hoping no one had seen them from the mansion.

A small grassy field separated the hedge from the garage. Will kneeled down to again check the tracking device. "It looks like Blake is in the back, on the bottom floor so we're going to go up the fire escape and sneak in through that top window. I want you both to stay behind me. Once I've got things covered, I'll need you both to help me carry them out if they can't walk."

The doctor suddenly interrupted, saying, "Will, if I get cut, you know that…"

"I know, Jay." Will sighed. "Just do what you can."

"Afraid of a little blood?" Catherine asked him.

The doctor ignored the question and kissed her on the cheek. "Whatever happens, I want you to know I'm sorry."

"Sorry?" Catherine touched a finger to the very spot he'd kissed.

"I know at times it might have appeared as if I was flirting with you, but the chemistry was only one sided. Will is far better for you than I ever could be."

"Whatever you say, Doc," Catharine agreed. "I just think you're keeping something from me, the real reason there can't be a relationship between us, even if there were mutual chemistry between us."

"I am," he admitted. "But now is not the place or the time to tell you. Just promise me something."

"What?" Catherine questioned.

"I realize that I invaded your privacy, but I did it with the best of intentions. I wanted to protect you and my Janet Network. Whatever you do, Catherine, if something should happen to me… don't bring down the Network. Think of the good this organization does. It has saved over a hundred women."

Catherine gazed deeply into the doctor's brilliant blue eyes. At first her anger showed and then her eyes softened. "All right. Since you're obviously sincere in your efforts to help abused women, I'll keep my objections to your methods to myself. I won't hurt the Network. You have my promise."

"Jay." Will clapped his hand to the doctor's shoulder. "Nothing bad is going to happen to you. Now, let's go."

The three of them ran from the hedge to the two-story garage. Luckily an armed guard they hadn't seen on top of the huge home until right then was looking in the direction of the driveway and failed to see them. Slowly, Will crawled up the fire escape ladder, followed by Catherine and the doctor. When they reached the top floor, Will and the doctor climbed onto the ledge and peered through a window down into the bowels of the building. The first floor housed several antique cars and motorcycles. Hayden and Blake were tied to chairs in the midst of the classic vehicles. Neither of them appeared to have been shot, but both were bleeding from the head. To the left was a staircase that led to the top story, where a mezzanine around the entire inside circumference of the building was cluttered with stored tools and boxes.

"They're beat up, pretty badly," the doctor observed. "That cut on Carl's head is going to need stitches. He may even have a concussion."

"First things first." Will slowly inched the window open. "Let's concentrate on getting them out of here first." Off in the distance, sirens began to wail. One of the two gunmen guarding Hayden and Blake looked up to spot Will climbing through the window. He yelled and pulled his gun, but Will fired first, taking the man down. Just as the other gunman took aim at Will, Jay began firing at him from the open window. The wounded gunman crawled behind a green sixty-nine Firebird and continued to fire at Will who'd taken cover behind a tool chest. He popped out to return fire as the second gunman darted toward Hayden. Just as the gunman raised his gun to the back of Hayden's head, Jay fired at him. The bullet hit the gunman in the chest, and he dropped hard onto the cement floor. He'd never shot a man before. Unconcerned he'd left himself out in the open, he went utterly still and stared at the pool of blood forming on the cement beneath the man he'd shot. The wounded gunman popped out from behind the Firebird and got off a shot at him before Will could put the man down. The gunman's bullet tore into Jay's right arm, and he fell back onto the fire escape, dropping his gun to clutch his arm.

"Doc!" Catherine screamed, moving to help him.

"No! Stop!" He held his bloody hand out, moving to kick at her to keep her back. "Stay away from me, Catherine!"

"What?" she gasped, as a half dozen police cars descended on the mansion and garage. "I need to help you."

"You can't help me, Catherine. Just stay back."

While four more gunmen rushed from the house toward the garage, an officer with a bullhorn ordered, "This is the Key West Police Department. Drop your weapons!"

Catherine ignored the melee around her as gunfire ensued between the police and the gunmen. "You're not making sense, Doc. Please let me help you." She inched forward.

"Will!" the doc roared, shocking her into stillness. "Get out here! I'm hit!" Breathing hard, he peered at Catherine, who stared at him now as if he were crazy. "I'm sorry, Catherine. You can't help me. Not with this."

"Why? We have to stop the bleeding." She ripped at her skirt to gather fabric for a tourniquet.

Will climbed out the window, grabbing her shoulders to push her back from the blood soaking the doctor's shirt and gathering around him on the windowsill and beneath it. "Did you touch him?" He shook her, pressing for an answer. "Do you have his blood on you anywhere?"

Catherine reeled with astonishment, and then anger set in. "What difference does that make? Let me go! He's bleeding! We need to help him," she cried, trying to break loose of Will's grip.

"Dammit, Catherine!" he shouted, shaking her again, harder this time. And he kept shaking her. "Do you have any of the doctor's blood on you?"

"Will!" Jay struggled to his feet. "Stop it! She's okay! She didn't touch me."

Will seemed to calm. He quit shaking her but shoved her back toward the ladder. "Go on. Climb down," he told her, his tone of voice brooking no argument as he took the strip of fabric from her and handed it to Jay. Catherine stared at him, and then gave the doctor a concerned look as he sluggishly tied the makeshift tourniquet around his arm. He was growing paler, and he appeared as if he might pass out.

"He'll be okay," he assured her. "Go on now."

"But I don't understand—"

The doctor leaned his head against the window frame. Barely able to speak, he looked right at Catherine and said, "Listen to Will."

"But you're bleeding so much!" Catherine fought the tears welling in her eyes.

"Just go down to the SUV and call me an ambulance from your cell phone. That's how you can help me, okay?"

Hayden's voice called out to Will from below. "Be right there!" he shouted back. He peered down at Catherine. "You heard him. Go." Although hesitantly, there wasn't much else she could do.

Will's stomach knotted as his eyes collided with his friend's. "I'm sorry, Jay," he said, his face haggard with worry.

"Never mind. Just do what you have to do. I'll be all right."

Will nodded and jumped back through the window, careful to let nothing but the soles of his shoes touch Jay's blood. He ran down the stairs, taking two or three at a time. When he got to the bottom he rushed across the room to Hayden and Blake. Pulling a knife from his back pocket, he cut Hayden's hands free and then handed him the blade.

Outside, the gunfire continued sporadically. "Let's go give the cops a hand."

"We've got your back." Hayden cut his legs free and hurried over to Blake to free him.

By the time Catherine returned to sit on the top step of the fire escape, she'd put two and two together and didn't like her conclusion. Nevertheless, she had to accept it. "So now I know," she said, staring at the doctor, "what the issue is."

Jay didn't move. He merely stared back at her. The tourniquet had slowed his bleeding but hadn't stopped it. He needed more pressure on the wound. And she couldn't provide it.

"You should have told me," she admonished him. "But that's so like you, isn't it? Being evasive has become such a habit for you that you show only part of the truth, while you hide behind a wall of your own secrets."

The doctor softly admitted, "I was worried about the Network. I couldn't be up front about it."

"Do you have any idea how much I care about you?" Catherine's eyes filled with tears. "To find out this way... I can't help my feelings. If anything happens to you..."

"You don't even know me, Catherine."

"I don't know you!" Catherine gasped, wanting desperately to stop his arm from continuing to bleed. "You've spent your life serving others, helping out the mentally ill and the emotionally distressed. You saved women from lives of abuse with your advice and guidance. I don't always agree with your methods, but know this, Doc, I respect you as a doctor and I adore you as a man. Everyone who speaks your name says it with reverence and appreciation for what you have done over so many years."

A weak smile crossed his lips. "You should've stayed in the SUV. It's safer there," he murmured as he slowly closed his eyes. "I feel so cold." And then he passed out.

Catherine clasped her hands together just as much to keep from reaching out to him as to say a silent prayer for him.

"Catherine!" Will called from down below. She said a soft "Amen," and then peered down at him.

"Hayden, Blake and I are going to assist the police with Miller's men. I want you to go back to the SUV and stay there."

"I'm not leaving Jay here alone!"

"You've done all you can for him. Now go!"

"No! I'm not leaving him!" Catherine reached over to pick up the gun which lay several feet from the doctor's body. There was no blood on the weapon. She showed it to Will below. "We'll be fine!"

Hayden, Blake and Will rushed through the back door of the garage and hid behind a dumpster. The police had surrounded the garage. In the center of the yard, officers were firing at four men on the mansion rooftop with AR- 15s. In a loud barrage of return fire, Miller's men returned fire, forcing the cops to take cover behind their car doors.

Distracted by the cops, the rooftop shooters didn't see Hayden, Blake and Will heading toward the back of the massive home. The three slowly climbed up the rain gutters and spread out behind the four shooters on the roof.

CHAPTER 44

With the doctor unconscious, Catherine was unable to deny her curiosity. She went back down the ladder and inched along the garage wall until she could see around the corner of the building. Hayden, Blake and Will had surrounded the four shooters on the roof. Two of the five gunmen were firing down onto the police below. Blake and Hayden kicked two off the roof. The third gunman turned, but Will grabbed the rifle out of his hands and punched him in the nose. Hayden shoved the fourth one over the ledge. He screamed and landed into the pool below.

"Doc, I wish you could see this," she said under her breath.

The last gunman tried to kick Will in the head. Ducking, Will punched the man in the stomach. The assailant landed on his back, grabbing his belly in agony.

In the distance, armored trucks with the words SWAT and DEA on the side were speeding down the road. Once the vehicles stopped, men poured out and broke down the front door to raid the mansion in one big swoop. Hayden and Blake jumped onto the balcony below. Blake kicked in the window, and they rushed in to assist in the assault.

"SWAT is a little late for the party, great job!" Catherine commented.

"We were never late for any parties, were we, darling?" The familiar voice came from behind Catherine.

Catherine whirled around, wishing she hadn't left the gun on the fire escape to climb down the ladder. Her ex-lover stood there, wearing a long black hooded sweat suit and black pants. He was holding a handgun on her.

"Lucky?"

"Have you missed me?" He flashed her a superior grin.

The small hairs on the back of Catherine's neck stirred. "Not particularly."

"Well, at least you remember my name," he replied. "Looks like your lover boy doctor didn't make out so well in the gunfight."

"The doctor isn't my lover," Catherine said, gulping hard. "I haven't been with anybody else since you left me."

"I left *you*?" He sneered. "Don't you have that a bit backwards? It wasn't me who brought the police to the Millers' door. It wasn't me who went to a shrink and ruined our lives!" Lucky spit out the words with contempt. "You've cost us millions. Not to mention we're shit deep in cops!"

Catherine gasped. "I didn't know what was going on or that you were into all of this!"

He moved toward her. "Would knowing have stopped you from wrecking everything? Would you have been loyal to me, knowing how much money I was really worth?" He halted in his tracks, and Catherine's eyes welled with tears.

"I'm not an idiot, Catherine." He ground the words out between clenched teeth. "It wouldn't have changed anything, and that's why I never told you. And now you know far too much to walk away unscathed. Believe me, this isn't what I wanted to happen. I loved you. Still do, but you've given me no choice." His hand shook as his finger tightened on the trigger. "You have to die, Catherine."

"Please… don't." She wept, tears pouring down her cheeks.

Catherine closed her eyes and screamed as a shot rang out. Her knees collapsed under her, and she landed on her butt, jolting her eyes open. Checking herself, she realized she hadn't been hit at all. Lucky, however, lay on the ground before her, bleeding from a wound to his back.

She peered up at the doctor. Having apparently crawled to where she'd left the gun, he lay on his stomach, stretched out along the fire escape. His eyes were barely open as he slowly lowered the gun. Catherine wanted to go to him, touch him, hold him, but all she could do was thank him for saving her life.

"My pleasure," he said, nodding at Lucky. "Is he dead?" Catherine knelt over Lucky and rolled him over. His eyes were closed, but he was breathing. She checked his throat. "He's got a faint pulse," she said.

"Good. He needs to testify against the Millers. They're the big fish here." Jay groaned and then and let his forehead drop to his good forearm.

"Are you all right, Doc? The ambulance is coming. Just hold on, a little longer."

He lifted his head and smiled weakly. "Where's Will?"

"Oh my God, Will!" Catherine couldn't believe she'd virtually forgotten about him. She ran back to the corner of the garage and peeked around it just in time to see Will throw a punch at the man he was still fighting on the roof. His attacker ducked the punch and let out a bloodcurdling cry as he ran at Will and forced him back against the railing around the top of the roof.

Concern furrowed her brow as the man began choking Will and tried to push him off the roof. The police below were trying to get a good shot at the man, but he kept pulling Will up to block any clear angle. Suddenly Will grabbed the man's hands and head-butted him backwards. Jumping up, he kicked the gunman hard in the knee, forcing his leg to buckle. The man went down, and Hayden emerged from the house with the Millers, the son and the older man with a cane. He helped an officer place them in the back of a long, black unmarked car.

Catherine announced, "Hayden has arrested the Millers."

Just then Blake ran back onto the rooftop. Together, he and Will handcuffed the hoodlum's hands behind his back.

"Will's captured the last of the shooters!" Catherine glanced back at the doctor, only to discover he had again passed out. She yelled out, "We need an ambulance over here! Fast!"

"The EMTs just got cleared to move in," Hayden shouted back.

Catherine saw the ambulances coming down the long driveway. Tears filled her eyes when she realized, they were all somehow still alive, at least so far. Her worries were focused on the doctor as the EMTs scaled the fire escape ladder.

"Hurry, please!" she cried. "He's been shot in the arm."

"And be careful," she warned. "He's HIV positive." Immediately, gloves came out and as the tourniquet was pulled off, blood poured from the wound.

"He's lost a lot of blood," one of the EMTs announced. "I'll radio ahead to have a transfusion ready. Looks like the bullet went right through and missed the humerous and major arteries."

"He'll be okay, right?" Catherine asked, expectantly.

The man smiled down at her. "He'll be in good hands at the hospital."

Will came up around the corner of the garage and wrapped an arm around Catherine's shoulders. Bloody trails from his facial cuts ran down his face. He had a fat lip, and one eye was swollen almost shut. He took the edge of his shirt and wiped the red streaks from his face.

"What does the other guy look like?" the other EMT asked him as he held up the IV bag to which the doctor had just been connected.

"Prettier than me." Will grinned.

"You want me to bandage you after the hooded guy?" the EMT questioned.

"Take care of that clown next." Will pointed to Lucky.

Catherine leaned against him and smoothed her thumb beneath his fat lip. "You have no idea how happy I am to see you're okay."

Will lowered his swollen lips down onto hers. They kissed for a moment and then Catherine melted into his arms. He pulled her closer, holding her tight against his masculine frame.

"You're amazing!" she breathed against his lips.

"So, when did Lucky show up?" Will wanted to know, as they both watched another EMT bringing in a stretcher for the Doctor.

"Not long after you left. Lucky snuck up behind me with a gun, threatened to kill me and Jay shot him."

Will watched as they lifted the doctor's motionless body onto the stretcher. Together the two EMTs carried him down the stairs as two more EMTs arrived to aid Lucky. "I wonder if Jay ever wished he could have shot Janet's husband?"

"Knowing Jay, the thought probably never even entered his mind," Will said, kissing Catherine again.

"So how did he become HIV positive?" Catherine asked.

"It was after Janet. He had a female patient who was delusional, and she bit him on the hand. Apparently, her husband regularly cheated on her with whores who used intravenous drugs. The hospital knew she had the disease, so they immediately started testing him. People can be pretty cruel. Everyone thought he caught it from a gay lover."

Catherine's eyes opened wide in shock. "What?"

"Jay's gay, Catherine."

Catherine took in a deep breath. "That's why he wasn't attracted to me. I would never have guessed."

"He's gay? Now it all makes sense."

Will's eyes tightened and then he pressed on. "Jay has a steady partner."

"Who?"

"His name's Stanley." Will smiled. "I've only met him a couple times. He's rather shy and reserved. They've been together about four years now."

"I don't know what to say about all this," Catherine said, confused.

"Well, if you have a problem with being Jay's friend or patient now, you need to tell me. I don't want anyone around Jay who doesn't accept who he is. He's been through enough."

"I can only imagine," she said.

"I know first-hand how many teens and adults he's helped over the years. He treats the handicapped, drug and alcohol users, the terminally ill and the disabled. I met him after I was kicked off the force. I was lost. Drinking too much. Heading down the wrong path, and I realized I needed some kind of guidance. Jay was recommended to me by a friend whose daughter he'd helped through the loss of her best friend. If I hadn't gone to see Jay when I did, I wouldn't be here right now. He's the one who suggested I become a private investigator, because of my love of police work. I sort of fell naturally into the Janet Network, but he's accomplished so much more than helping abused women. This bust is another notch on his belt. Think about how many drugs we've all just helped the police keep off the streets!"

"You admire him."

"Anyone who doesn't, doesn't have a chance with me. Do you understand what I'm saying?" he asked with staid seriousness.

"Yes. You made that perfectly clear," she said, inching closer. "I find your loyalty and dedication to Jay a very appealing part of who you are."

"Catherine, I have feelings for you. I haven't made that a secret, either. I'd like to see where things go between us. I know you'll probably be in therapy for a while over what happened with Lucky, but I'm here for you as a friend or whatever else you need me to be."

"Whatever else?"

A smile crossed her lips. "I'm not one to run from a challenge."

"Is that how you see me," she questioned, "as a challenge?"

"When I look at you, I just know we'd be great together," he admitted. "It makes me wonder how you could ever have been involved with Lucky unless you had to be with him to meet me." He watched the EMTs hustle the still unconscious Lucky off on his stretcher.

Catherine admitted, "My past affects who I am. I'm not sure how ready I am to start dating."

"Make your past into a strength, not a weakness." Catherine nodded in agreement.

One of the EMTs came back. "All right," he said to Will, "it's your turn. You're going to walk out of here on your own or on a stretcher. Either way you're going to the hospital to have those facial cuts looked after."

"I'll walk to the ambulance." Will glanced at Catherine. "Care to join me for a little ride to the hospital?"

Gazing deeply into his dark hazel eyes, one of which was barely visible behind its swollen lid, she kissed his firm lips. Fire soared through every part of her, down to her core. She had never felt so drawn to a man or felt so protected as she did right now, standing next to her sexy, Italian stallion. Her heart rejoiced as she reached out and lovingly held his big hand. "Sounds romantic."

CHAPTER 45

As Catherine walked into the hospital room, her eyes widened at the enormous collection of flowers and balloons that surrounded Jay's bed. After she counted several dozen rose bouquets, two giant stuffed animals, a bear and a tall giraffe with "Get Well" helium balloons tied to its legs, she stopped counting.

"Doc," Catherine said, greeting him by the bed. "It's hard to find you among these animals and flowers this morning."

"Margie, my secretary, blurted out to a few of my patients that I had been admitted to the hospital. It appears I'm a bit spoiled." He sat up, slowly. His arm was bandaged from the shoulder to the elbow.

"Your color is returning."

"I heard you stayed and kept checking on Will and me most of the night." The doctor smiled.

"Will is taking the hospital stay much harder than you. He tried leaving twice last night; he's already bored. Hopefully, he'll be released this morning when the ER doctor arrives for his morning rounds."

"How many stitches?"

"Will counted 23 over five major leg and arm cuts, 10 bruises and 12 more stitches above the right eye," Catherine announced. "He's claiming they are all worth it."

The doctor glanced over her. "You look radiant."

"Around 4:00 a.m. I went to the motel, showered and then took a brief nap before coming back to see if either of you needed a ride home."

"They're keeping me for another night of further observation," the doctor said.

Catherine moved over to the stuffed giraffe and petted its head. "This is really cute."

"You like giraffes?" he asked. "You know you can feed them at the local zoo. Will should take you some time."

"Yes, I think I'll ask him to do that." She smiled.

"Have you heard anything about Lucky?" His tone darkened.

"I did overhear from a police officer that he's going to live," Catherine informed.

"Good." The doctor sighed, then leaned his head back onto the pillow. "I really didn't want blood on my hands twice."

"You saved my life again." Catherine sat down on the edge of the bed. "I don't know how to ever thank you."

"I'll think of something." The doctor grinned mischievously.

"You have no idea how horrible it was to see you covered in blood," Catherine admitted. "For a while you didn't move, and I feared I'd lose my doc."

He squeezed her hand. "Are you still angry with me?"

"If it wasn't for your help, I think I'd be a lot worse off. Will thinks of you and your Janet Network as some sort of heroic endeavor."

"Heroic? Well I have been known to leap over piles of designer clothes to find a good sale; does that classify me as a superhero?"

"I don't think so," Catherine said wryly.

"Well, someday you'll realize that I was only doing what I thought necessary to save you from yourself. And from Lucky."

She gently hugged his right side and kissed him on the cheek. The doctor didn't push her away; instead he raised his uninjured arm to embrace her.

"I suppose since you know about my chronic illness now you figured out what our issue is for not dating."

Gently, she ran her fingers through his gray-blond hair, gazing into the blue pools of his eyes. "The HIV couldn't have kept me from dating you. It was the fact you're gay and didn't desire me back. That was the issue."

Jay gazed candidly at her. "I can't deny it." "Besides, my heart has already been taken."

"Mine too."

"Excuse me." Hayden came in, wearing only a hospital gown. His hair was wet and combed back.

"You, again?" The doctor grimaced, releasing Catherine from the hug. "You just missed my sponge bath. Your timing must be off today."

"I've seen enough." Hayden laughed. "I thought I would let you both know the latest. So far, one of Miller's four sons is still in critical condition with concussion and gunshot wound to the leg, but even he looks as if he'll pull through. Lucky is stable. The bullet was removed but it broke two of his ribs. Three police officers were shot, and all three made it out of surgery okay. Will is in good enough condition to be a pain in the butt. We've made fifteen arrests in the case and found over a quarter of a million dollars worth of cocaine in the icehouse. We confiscated seven trucks, twenty-six guns, ten foreign sports cars, three jets, two boats and a yacht, then found nearly twelve million dollars in Millers wall safe, along with several shipments of pot. If the Millers are found guilty of trafficking in drugs, which is pretty much a certainty, especially if Lucky turns state's evidence, all property will be sold, and the funds used to further the DEA's anti-drug operations in Florida. All in all, I'd say the FBI, DEA and ATF had one hell of a great day."

"You are forgetting one thing," the doctor added. "Catherine is free of one abusive son-of-a-bitch. She can live her own life as she chooses and not be afraid of bodily harm."

"Yeah, and that too." Hayden limped closer and shook the doctor's hand. "Thank you for everything you did. I'm just sorry you got shot in the process."

"Looks like you got hurt too." The doctor nodded at his leg.

"Ah, it's just a bruised knee," Hayden explained. "Lucky kicked me when I was tied up."

"And Blake," Catherine wanted to know. "How is he?"

"He's on the third floor. The second-floor nurses took his skateboard away because he was skating down the hall with just a robe on. The younger nurses didn't seem to mind as long as there were no patients around, but one of the older ladies made him change floors because she said, 'His skinny legs bothered her'. Overall, he's got a minor eye and facial wound and lots of stitches on one leg. He'll be fine. Maybe one more night in the hospital. He'll make the games and probably win a trophy or two. Again, I'm sure."

Catherine chuckled. "Sounds like Blake."

A knock sounded at the door. Hayden turned around to see who was standing there, and then immediately headed out the door. "If there's more news, I'll keep you posted."

"Thanks, Hayden," the doctor replied.

Catherine didn't know the handsome stranger at the door, but she didn't need to be introduced to see the tears shining in the man's stunning green eyes. He was thin, attractive and had a balloon in one hand which read, "I love you."

"Stanley?" Catherine asked him.

He nodded in the affirmative and moved toward the bed. Catherine rose to leave, but before she did, she leaned over and kissed the doctor on the cheek. "See you soon."

"Goodbye, Catherine."

At the door, she glanced back, only to discover Stanley sitting on the bed, wiping his tears. She waved goodbye with a smile, surmising Stanley would rather spend some time with the doctor alone.

CHAPTER 46

Will was glad to see the hospital door swing closed behind him as he was wheeled toward the passenger side of the green SUV waiting for him. Catherine rushed from behind the wheel to help the nurse open the passenger door. Will didn't wait for the nurse to set the brakes on his wheelchair before he jumped out of it and slid into the vehicle.

"That one sure is anxious to get home," the nurse murmured to Catherine.

"You can say that again. Thank you for everything." Catherine smiled, and then hurried back to the driver's seat.

"Get me out of here," Will pleaded. "If I see any more women in scrubs today I'm going to scream."

Grinning, Catherine restarted the engine and pulled away from the curb in front of the hospital's main entrance. "You know, I've been thinking about buying a couple pairs of scrubs. They look so comfortable for around the house."

"Don't you dare." He gave her a look numb with horror.

She burst out laughing. "I'm just kidding. I just wanted to see that look on your face."

"What look?"

"Oh, the one that says *if you wear scrubs around me, I'm going to go certifiably insane because it reminds you of being stuck in a hospital.*"

"Well, it's true."

"I know." Her eyes danced as she slid him a radiant smile. "So where am I taking you?"

Will fingered the stitches above one eye. "I have a nice apartment downtown, three bedrooms with a great view overlooking the river. The walls are gold and trimmed with garnet because I have lots of Florida State stuff. That's where I earned my Bachelor of Criminology degree."

"FSU is a very prestigious college."

"I got my education at Eastern Florida State College."

"Take the interstate about six miles and then take the nineteen-ten exit. It's not far from Castle Builders," Will told her.

Catherine turned onto the freeway and as they approached a sign reading, *ZOO, New Reptile Show Saturday & Sunday Only, Next Exit*, she pointed at it. "Doc mentioned we should check out the zoo sometime, because they have a large giraffe exhibit. I love giraffes."

"You can feed them." Will suddenly grinned. "Let's go."

"Now? You need to rest."

"No, I don't. That's all I've done in the hospital. A nice long walk around the animal park sounds like fun, especially if we're together." Will reached out and took her hand.

Catherine shrugged. "Why not then?" She took her hand back from Will and exited the freeway. She drove past the zoo sign and headed into a dirt parking lot near the entrance.

"You afraid of snakes?" Will exited the truck after they parked and then rushed around to open Catherine's door.

"I love them. My childhood neighbor was a science teacher and had this twelve-foot python in his garage. It ate rats."

"After what we've been through, I'd say we've already conquered a few of our own snakes." She hopped out of the truck and took his hand. They got in line at the ticket booth, and when they got to the window, Will paid for their tickets, two lunch passes and the train ride around the zoo.

"This is going to be fun!" Catherine grinned.

"We deserve some of that." Will guided her into the giant park.

She was handed a map by a zoo employee. Taking a look, she decided immediately that she wanted to see the giraffes first. Will was looking over her shoulder and saw what she was pointing to.

"We'll have to pass the reptile show to get there."

"I'm game." She smiled eagerly. "What do you feed the giraffes anyway?"

"Some sort of cracker that looks like packaged hay." Will suddenly stopped in front of a giant cage. Inside was an enormous lizard about five feet in length with spikes coming out of his head and long unusual fingers that were clasping a fat branch.

"An iguana!" Catherine exclaimed, delighted. "I haven't seen one since I was a kid."

"It looks like a mini dragon, doesn't it?"

"I used to have one as a pet," Catherine informed him. "His name was Jamison, and he was the smartest lizard any girl could ever have."

"Smart?" He looked skeptical. "A lizard?"

"He was almost that big." She smiled, nodding at the one in the cage. "And he was incredibly smart. I even taught him how to use a litter box."

"You've got to be kidding."

"I loved him very much. I miss him, still."

"I didn't even know iguanas made good pets." Will waited until Catherine moved down to the next cage, that of a giant turtle.

"Now that's a huge amphibian," Will announced, then he saw the walkway. "This way to the giraffes. We can see the rest of the reptiles later."

Catherine hurried to keep pace. "I can't wait."

They walked up a large slope to a wooden building open on one side. Three tall giraffes peered over the railing at the several children who were reaching up, offering them crackers.

Will picked up four from a concession stand and headed toward the giant animals. "Here." He handed Catherine one. "You go first."

Trembling a bit, she moved closer. The giant head swung around toward her, and with a long black tongue, grabbed the treat and pulled it into its mouth. Catherine petted its head and then it moved lower to get another edible square from a boy.

"This is absolutely awesome!"

Will moved toward the smallest of the three giraffes but waited until Catherine stood next to him so she could pet its head while it ate the cracker from his hand. "Aren't they beautiful?"

"They are the most unique and incredible creatures on earth."

"This one is the baby of the three and he comes all the way from Africa. He was injured by hyenas when he was born. See the bite mark on its left leg?"

Catherine looked and noticed the scar between the orange spots covering his leg. "It's a miracle he survived."

Will suddenly whirled her into his arms and Catherine curled her arms around Will's neck as he kissed her. He ran his tongue slowly over her lips, and she dissolved in his embrace, her toes threatening to curl in ecstasy. The giraffes were there and when one poked its head between them, trying to get at the last two crackers in Catherine's hand, she pulled back from the kiss, laughing.

"Couldn't you have waited just few more minutes?" Will said to the giraffe. "I was getting some good lovin' here."

Catherine gave the giraffe the other two crackers and then she turned on a heel and got on the tips of her toes. Her mouth gently touched Will's, and while the giraffes watched and the children giggled, the couple embraced in a long, passionate kiss that felt as if it might last an eternity.

CHAPTER 47

Jay walked through the double doors into the surgical waiting room, immediately spotting Catherine, sitting next to a lovely older woman who told him a lot about what Catherine would look like in a few years. He wasn't on duty, but Catherine wouldn't know that.

He approached, watching the two women clutching hands and praying. He had seen many people implore a higher power to facilitate their surgery beforehand. He'd never thought much of it, but this time it got to him.

This time was different, more personal. Closer to home for him. He personally knew and cared about the people involved and what it meant if Doctor Harold Burrows couldn't remove all the cancerous tissue. Catherine needed her mother more than ever. From what he'd read from surveillance notes, they were very close and clung together in times of trial and tragedy. He had even heard a rumor that it had been Catherine's mother who had referred her daughter to him through a friend's recommendation.

When Marla Walters ended her prayer and opened her eyes, they widened. "Well now, if doctors all looked like this handsome young man, I'd come to the hospital more often," her mother joked, her expression brightening as she peered up at Jay.

Catherine's eyes glinted with pleasure as she took Jay's hand in hers and squeezed. "Mom, this is Dr. Jay Newport."

"The man who saved you from Lucky?" her mother asked, her voice tremulous with emotion. "I owe so much, Dr. Newport. Thank you so much for all you've done for my daughter."

The doctor smiled. "It's nice to meet you, Mrs. Walters."

"Call me Marla," her mother said.

"How's your arm?" Catherine noticed he wasn't wearing a sling. "Where is your sling?"

"I'm doing fine without it," the doctor lied.

"Working?" Catherine asked. "Only a few days released and he's already back to saving lives, Mom."

"You exaggerate terribly." The doctor grinned.

"No, I really don't." Catherine cocked her head. "I can't thank you enough for everything."

"Well I'm on call; I'd better be going," he lied. "I just wanted to wish your mom all the best and make sure you were doing okay."

"Can't you stay?" her mother asked. "My daughter really needs someone to sit with her, especially if the news is bad."

"Now I don't want you thinking that way, Mrs. Walters. This is a very simple procedure, and I know you'll both be very pleased with the outcome."

"Is he always this positive?" her mother asked Catherine.

"Yes." Catherine chuckled.

Suddenly the hospital room door opened and in walked Will carrying a bushel of yellow roses. "Will!" The doctor's eyes showed his surprise, a reaction not without a little trepidation. He had just been caught. Will knew that he had taken two weeks off from work to recover from the shooting. "I was just making rounds and thought I would stop by to wish Mrs. Walters well."

Will gave him a quick look, telling him he would cover his little lie. "It's nice that you came to see Catherine and her mother since you are so busy."

"Yes, I must be going." He gave Marla a quick nod and smile before he hurried back out through the doors.

"I wish he could stay too." Catherine sighed.

"These are for you, Mrs. Walters," Will said, "but I'll hang onto them for you until you're out of recovery."

"Oh, they're very lovely. Thank you." Marla reached up and touched a bloom. She leaned forward to smell their wonderful fragrance.

"Anything for Catherine's mom," he said, smiling.

"And you, young man, must be this Will Cilva, Private Investigator, I've been hearing all about."

"Mom," Catherine gasped, embarrassed.

Her mother raised a brow. "I really do need to hang out in the hospital more often," she chortled, for her daughter's ears only.

Will chuckled, deep in his throat, just as a nurse, with a file folder in her hand, pushed through the inner set of double doors and called out Marla's name.

Her mother grabbed her right breast through her gown and threw her other arm in mock tribulation across her brow. "Goodbye, Girlfriend. It's been nice knowing you."

Catherine and Will started laughing. "Mom, you are so out there."
"Well, it's better than crying."

"Yes, it is, Mrs. Walters," Will agreed.

"Please," she said, getting up from her chair, "call me Marla." Winking at him, she and Catherine hugged, and then she went with the nurse.

As soon as they disappeared through the doors to the inner sactum, tears began to stream down Catherine's cheeks. Will immediately held her in his arms. "It's okay, Catherine. It's going to be okay."

He held her in his arms until her sniffles ceased. "How long will you be able to stay?" she asked.

"I'll be here as long as you want. I took the day off."

"You did?"

He was glad Catherine seemed so pleased. "Where else would I be?" Will smiled.

"Thank you."

"Can I get you a drink?" Will asked.

"Not now, thanks," Catherine said. "The doctor informed my mom that the operation would take at least an hour."

"That's not bad." Will laid the roses down on the sofa beside Catherine and went to where a few soda and snack machines were lined up against the wall. He ran a dollar bill into a machine and hit the grape soda button. A quarter plinked into the change back bin. He scooped it out and opened the can tab to take a slurp. "Look we've got a television," he said, sliding the flowers over so he could sit beside Catherine. "We'll just hang out and watch a few game shows until we get word."

"They'll come and get us, right?"

"Of course." Will mustered up the courage to put his arm around Catherine's shoulders. "We'll know soon how your mom's doing."

But time dragged slowly by. Will could have counted how many zits were on the contestants' faces. The game show was about as exciting as watching worms wrestle. Still, he didn't move. He kept his arm around Catherine. She hadn't been paying attention at all. Her eyes were fixated on the floor while she took deep calming breaths.

When the door finally opened, a man wearing a white coat approached. Catherine rose to her feet and Will followed suit. He guessed that the tall, chubby, blond man who appeared to be in his mid-thirties was Marla's doctor.

"Catherine Walters?" Doctor Burrows cracked a smile. "I believe I have successfully removed all the cancerous tissue in your mother's right breast."

Catherine nearly collapsed. She sat back down, tears of relief beginning to stream down her cheeks.

Dr. Burrows reached out and patted her on the back. "Your mother will be just fine. She'll be in recovery for about an hour and then I'll have a nurse come get you."

"Thank you, Doctor." Will stuck his hand out and the doctor shook it. He smiled one more time at Catherine and then strolled out of the waiting room to speak to a nurse in the hallway.

"It's over, sweetheart." Will sat back down and pulled Catherine into his arms. "Your mom is going to be just fine."

Catherine wiped her eyes on his shirt. "I know Dr. Burrows just said so, but something could still happen in recovery."

"Catherine," he interrupted her, putting her out at arm's distance to get her full attention, "what are you doing? Other than the cancer, your mother's healthy, right?"

"Well, yes."

"Then don't borrow trouble. They got the cancer out. And that's what matters."

CHAPTER 48

Will and Catherine entered the crowded skate park filled with custom halfpipes, rails and grind boxes. Television cameras were pointed at the skaters as they took turns, fighting for the highest points to win the championship. The crowd applauded the moment they announced the name of the next competitor to skate: "Blake Anderson."

Catherine began to pull Will forward by the hand. "Come on. We're going to miss him."

"Hold your horses." Will rushed after her.

They practically ran to the stadium seating and stood in awe as Blake skated up a ramp, performed a quick Ollie, and then spun 360 degrees with a kickflip.

"Will!" someone from the stands cried out.

Catherine turned her head and discovered several people in the crowd were calling them to come stand beside them to watch the rest of Blake carve his way through the course. "Who are they?" she asked.

"That's my secretary on the right. Fred is one of my men and to the left of him is Blake's girlfriend."

"Wow, she's gorgeous." With long blonde hair, a dark tan and an incredible athletic build, Catherine thought Blake's girlfriend looked like a professional model.

"She's a bikini model," Will confirmed.

Catherine turned her attention back to Blake who had just finished doing a treflip and then the very difficult triple kickflip. The audience was going crazy. They were standing on their feet, clapping and chanting, "Blake, Blake, Blake…"

On the big screen above the halfpipe, they flashed Blake's smiling skull face and his score. He was in the lead with only two more competitors to go. Blake jumped off his board at the top of the halfpipe, grabbed his board in midair and landed on his feet to take a bow as the audience continued cheering, hooting, and blowing horns.

Blake watched the next few skaters attempt what he had just achieved and then over the loudspeaker, the announcement was made: "Blake Anderson has won the Game-X Championship for the State of Florida. This makes it his second gold medal."

An unopened can of soda suddenly crashed to the floor beside Catherine. Lucky it hadn't hit her, much less burst open to drench her in sticky soda. She glanced up to see who had thrown the can at her. Among the many spectators in the stands, she saw a flash of bright red hair. *Abby, Lucky's sister?* she wondered.

"Where did that come from?" Will frowned as he scanned the crowd.

"Look there!" Catherine pointed up into the stands. "That woman running up the steps—the one with red hair; she has a hat on—I think she threw it."

His eyes searched until he found the woman Catherine was talking about. He rushed after her, with Fred in his wake. A hand on her shoulder startled Catherine, and she whirled around to discover Blake's girlfriend. "Who threw that?" she asked. "Should I go tell Blake?"

Catherine saw that Blake was being handed his championship medal. "Not now. It might have even been an accident. I think Will just went to see who had done it."

"You're Catherine, Will's girlfriend, right?"

A smile crossed Catherine's face. "I suppose." She hadn't really thought of herself as that, but she supposed that was exactly what she had become since they seemed to have been going out on a regular basis.

"I'm Blake's girlfriend," she announced. "It's nice to meet you."

"Congratulations on Blake's win." Catherine flashed her a knowing smile. "I had a feeling he would win."

"Are you kidding? If he hadn't, we would never hear the end of it." She laughed. "This is all he's been training for. Next is the surf competition in Daytona. I'm going to enter the bikini contest there. It should be a really great weekend. You two should come along."

Catherine glanced back at Blake. He was so proud, holding the trophy in one hand and signing autographs with the other. "That sounds like fun. I'll talk to Will."

"Great!"

Will was heading back down the steps. By the frustration on his face, Catherine could tell he hadn't caught up to the red-haired woman.

"I couldn't catch her. She ran up and back down the side aisle to the parking lot. Fred is talking to the parking lot security to see if they have any cameras. If they don't, we'll never know who she is and why she threw that bottle at your head."

"It might have been an accident," Catherine said. Will sighed.

"Somehow, I doubt that."

CHAPTER 49

Catherine knew her mother had agreed to take her in, but would she *really* be pleased that her grown daughter was moving back in?

In her mother's driveway, Will opened the pick-up door for her. "Why don't you just move in with me?"

Their eyes locked and she stared at him, barely able to believe he'd asked her such a thing so soon in their relationship. A tingling sensation nearly curled her toes. Desire soared through her veins with the very thought of living with such an amazing man. "That's very sweet of you to ask, but—"

"I make great pancakes," he bragged, grinning broadly.

"We'll see," Catherine promised with a bit more reserved smile.

He leaned over and kissed her lips. "Are you sure living with your mom is what you want?"

"Yes," Catherine said. "For now, anyway. She's recovering from surgery, and I think it would be best if I were here for her right now."

"Okay." Will took her hand and helped her down from the truck, where he swept her in his arms for several minutes.

Suddenly the front door opened, and her mother threw her hands up in the air. "Oh, this is fantastic! You're moving home to take care of your mother in her old age."

"Oh, stop!" Catherine knew her mother was joking.

"Can I help with any bags?" Her mother checked over the front seat and discovered only one bag on the floor. "Where are all of your things?"

"Seized by the Florida Drug Enforcement Agency," Will announced. "Turns out everything in Lucky's house was stolen and is about to be sold."

"Can't you fight it?" her mother wondered. "Those are your clothes!"

"It's not worth it," Catherine said.

"No, we should get you a lawyer," her mother pressed. "That isn't fair. You didn't sell any drugs."

"I don't want a thing that Lucky bought me," Catherine argued. "It would just remind me of him, and I don't want to think or talk about Lucky ever again."

Her mother's smile faded. "I understand, honey." She swung the front door wide. "Come right in. You can take the bedroom on the right. It has its own bathroom."

Will picked up the bag and followed Catharine up the walk. When she stopped on the porch, Will asked her, "You okay?"

"Yes. It's just that I feel like I'm walking out of one life and into another."

"That's a good thing…" Will grinned, "…as long as I'm a part of your new life."

"What do you see in me, Will?" Catherine asked him, truly puzzled. "I'm still so amazed we are dating."

"What don't I see?" Will leaned over and kissed her forehead. "You're a beautiful woman with a gentle soul who stole my heart."

"I stole your heart?" Her eyes welled with tears.

"Yes, you did," Will admitted. "The moment I saw you in that club. I couldn't believe you were Jay's new Janet."

"I'm not Janet anymore." Catherine gave him a triumphant smile. "I've come a long way in a very short time."

"Yes you have, and you have no idea how proud Jay and I are of you." Catherine looked surprised.

"The doctor's proud of me?"

"That's what he said when I talked to him yesterday. He invited us out on his boat for a quick trip down the river, but I told him that you were moving in with your mom today."

"Oh, I wish I would have known. I could have stayed another day at the motel so we could go."

"We'll go another time," Will said.

"I hope so." Catherine smiled. "I really care about him and what he thinks. I'm wondering in fact what he thinks about my moving."

"What do you mean?"

"I'm concerned Doc will think that it was a step backward. Here I am a middle-aged woman moving back in with my mommy."

"Actually, Jay thinks it's a step forward."

"He said that?" Catherine sounded surprised.

"Of course! Do you really think he wants you to keep staying in that motel? He was glad that you were moving in with your mom."

"Good." Catherine stepped in at the doorway. "This does seem like what I need to do to keep heading in the right direction."

CHAPTER 50

Jay greeted Catherine as she strolled into his office. "According to your chart it's been six months since I needed to prescribe a medication for you. How are you?"

She sat down on the chair opposite his desk. "The counselor you recommended, Darla Hennings, has really helped. I took her building self- esteem classes and things have gotten better with Mom now that we know her cancer was removed."

"You didn't need to make an appointment to see me." He smiled. "I would have come by your mother's. Will told me on our last fishing trip that you had moved in with her."

"Yes, and it's been nice spending time with her. How's Stanley?"

"Wonderful," the doctor informed her, leaning in his chair. "His father's birthday is tomorrow so we're heading over to Tampa for the weekend."

"Please tell him I said hello."

"Of course. Now, what's on your mind?"

"I've been a little nervous lately," Catherine admitted. "I was hoping that you could give me some more of your incredible advice and maybe another refill."

"What's going on?" the doctor questioned, worriedly. "Are you feeling overwhelmed again? I thought we had gotten a handle on your anxiety condition."

"Will asked me to marry him and now I have this big wedding to plan. I've been meeting with all these wedding planners and the whole thing is just stressing me out." She fiddled with her blouse cuff.

"Are you ready for this kind of commitment with Will?" Suddenly, Catherine burst into tears.

The doctor rose from his chair and sat closer to her on the edge of his desk. He placed a hand on her shoulder.

"I'm scared," she cried. "I love him, but I always have picked the wrong guys in the past. I don't know. He just seems too good to be true."

"And why is that?" the doctor inquired.

"I'm just too happy!" Her hands went to her eyes, wiping the flowing tears. "It's so scary being this happy."

"You haven't been happy in a long time, have you?"

"Not since I was young and living with my mother. I felt so at ease with Will when we were dating and now, he throws this marriage thing into the mix."

"Did you tell him you feel rushed?"

"I want to marry him," Catherine said. "It's just I always do the wrong thing. What if this is just that?"

"You've come a long way, Catherine. You've dealt with a lot of your past problems with your counselor. I'm sure Darla explored why you kept rushing into your previous relationships with dangerous men. Will is different from them. He's in control of his emotions and quite frankly, treats you very well. You're not used to that."

"I don't feel like I deserve him." She wiped her tears.

"You deserve all the happiness in the world," he said with a reassuring smile.

"So do you," Catherine put forward. "Look at you and Stanley. It's just not fair that you have to live with the threat of AIDS!"

The doctor leaned over her, handing her a box of tissues. "Catherine, if I only have one more year with Stanley, I'd rather have that one year and enjoy every minute of being in love than spend a lifetime with someone I don't love."

She began to weep harder. "That's so sweet!"

"Do you love Will, Catherine? Answer me honestly."

"With all my heart. I don't know why I am so scared."

"Part of this fear is natural. There is such a thing as cold feet, you know."

"The penguin-toe-itis, that's what I have. Is there a cure?"

The doctor laughed. "Yes, you need to try some of these relaxation techniques." He pulled a sheet of paper from a folder on his desk and handed it to her. Plus…" Picking up his prescription pad, he wrote out a refill and handed it to her. "…I want you to keep reminding yourself that Will is nothing like Lucky."

Catherine rose and hugged him. "I don't know what I would do without you."

The doctor smiled. "Remember when you said you would like to thank me, and I told you that I would think of something?"

"Yes." Catherine cocked her head and gave him an arch smile. "What do you want me to do? Your laundry or wash your car."

He chuckled. "No, although, my convertible does need a wash."

"Then what?"

"I'll let you know by the wedding, okay? Just as long as I can hold you to the one favor."

"Are you kidding? You can hold me to ten favors after what I'm about to ask of you."

"Ask away. Anything you want, it's yours," the doctor reassured her.

"Will you walk me down the aisle?" Catherine's eyes softened. "You've meant so much to me and I would really want you to be a part of the biggest day of my life."

"I can do that," the doctor agreed with a huge grin.

"Will is going to ask you to stand up for him, too."

"I can do that, too," the doctor added. "Anything else? I make a fancy vegetable cheese dip."

"We've got caterers for that." She laughed. "Monkey suit?"

"Yes, Will is ordering the rentals and scheduling an outdoor orchestra for part of the reception. Does Stanley do ballroom?"

"No, Stan doesn't dance. I, on the other hand, watch Dancing with the Stars and relish two dances, the rumba and the tango. The tango I do only for very special occasions."

"Well, Stanley is certainly invited."

"Stan has a thing about weddings," the doctor said, "but I'll let him know and tell him you asked specifically for his presence."

Catherine slowly walked toward the door, allowing the doctor to open it for her.

"So, I just need to relax and recognize having cold feet is natural."

"Yes," the doctor reiterated. "Frankly, I'm very happy for you both. I've known Will for years and have never seen him so head-over-heels in love. On our fishing trip, you were all he talked about."

"This is the real deal, isn't it?"

"I believe so." The doctor grinned.

"It feels that way." Catherine wiped her eyes. "I honestly enjoy my job. My bills are all paid, and I love my future husband. Everything else is just falling into place. It feels like I'm on a different planet."

"Happiness suits you." The doctor gave her a quick hug. "If you need me, call me, anytime, Catherine."

"You're on my speed dial."

"Catherine," the doctor added as she headed out the door, "congratulations! I'm looking forward to the happy nuptials."

CHAPTER 51

Bells chimed outside the small, white, wooden church. The doctor walked past several giant oak trees and up a few steps to the double arched doors. They were propped open by flower stands full of long stem white roses. Wearing a black tuxedo with full dress-tails and wool pleated pants, he checked the single white rose in his lapel. After making sure the bud was straight, he moved into the church to mingle among the guests.

So much time had passed since he had followed Catherine inside this small sanctuary and watched her light a single candle. Briefly, he glanced over the wooden pews to where she had knelt so long ago. She had prayed for him there and touched his heart in a way no other woman of the Janet Network had.

He breathed deeply, fighting nervousness, working toward fully controlling himself. As he quitted his beating heart, he observed the old wooden sanctuary with its colorful stained glass windows and the giant white rose bouquet on top of the altar. The roses were unique. In the center of each bloom was a yellow hue, and every petal had a slight pink edging. As he watched, the bridesmaids moved into their positions at the altar. The three bridesmaids were Catharine's cousins, and her Matron of Honor was an old friend from high school.

With a slow turn of a brightly polished leather shoe, he nodded his greetings to several guests being ushered to their seats until a familiar woman in a purple dress caught his attention. She was being escorted to her seat by one of the ushers, Leonardo Walters, Catherine's cousin. A short balding man with a large belly, Jay had met him at the wedding rehearsal and dinner the night before.

Leonard turned to him and smiled. "Doctor, Marla asked me to tell you that Catherine is ready and waiting for you. We're about to begin in a few minutes. She's in the room marked eight on the right. I'll knock on the door when it's time to start walking her down the aisle."

"Thank you, Leonard."

As Jay made his way back to the Bride's Room through a side hallway, he ran into Will and Catherine's Pastor, Reverend Jessie Myers. The thin, bearded minister turned from speaking to a teenager toward the doctor. His glasses dropped down his nose as he peered down from his over six-foot height. "Hello, Dr. Newport."

"Good afternoon, Pastor." The doctor shook his hand. "It's a pleasure to see you again." He and Jay had met just the night before at the rehearsal. "Are you ready for the big day?" he asked, pressing his glasses back up on his large nose.

"All set, Reverend."

"Good deal. Just like last night, Leonardo will knock on the door once Will and his groomsmen are situated at the front of the church. Once you hear the 'Wedding March', just begin to walk Catherine down at a slow pace. And Will's niece will be tossing red rose petals in front of you both for real this time."

"Very exciting," the doctor admitted.

"Yes, it is. Remember now, once you walk Catherine to the front of the church, I'll ask you to hand her over to Will and you just answer or nod yes. Then go stand beside the groomsmen and enjoy the rest of the wedding."

"Thank you for going over the instructions again for me," the doctor said. "I will try to do my best not to trip."

"You'll do fine," he said as he started down the hall with the young man. "Just go on into Catherine now," he threw back over his shoulder. "She's waiting in room eight for you."

The doctor immediately turned and paced down the corridor, watching the numbers on the doors until he arrived at number eight, Choir Room. He knocked and waited until he heard her ask, "Will? Leonardo?"

"It's me, Catherine."

She opened the door and her eyes lit up the second she saw him. "Hi, Doc!"

For a moment his breath caught in his throat. Catherine shone like an angel in a stunning white A-line satin and chiffon gown with a flowing seven-foot train. Her beaded bodice and the pearl appliqués on her gown glistened like morning dewdrops. She wore a single strand of pearls which matched the pearl tiara on her head. He couldn't speak he was so overwhelmed. Tears hovered in his eyes.

"I guess I look all right then?" She tried not to cry.

"That gown will do fine," he said, admiringly.

"Are they ready for us yet?" she wondered.

"Just waiting for Leonardo's knock."

"It's amazing so many of our families flew in for the wedding. My mother is here too! She's feeling so much better."

"I really enjoyed talking to her at dinner last night." The doctor's smile evaporated. "Do you know Sandra Peters?"

"Yes, she's a friend of Will's aunt Aggie. Why?" Catherine walked to the mirror and began to touch up her lipstick.

"She's that personal favor I need to ask you," the doctor said. "I didn't ask you before, but I would like to know, instead of just being one of my ex-Janets, would you like to join the Network?"

She lowered her lipstick, gazing at him in the mirror. "Sandra's husband Arnie hits her?"

"Can you keep this in confidence?"

"Absolutely," Catherine promised. "You have my word."

"There might be hope for Arnie. His anger problem seems to be connected with an underlying panic disorder and a childhood of past abuse. It may be correctable with medication and long-term counseling. He has agreed to therapy which is a positive thing. I always try my best to save the marriage before calling in the Network. However, Sandra may need some space. They also are having financial problems which are adding to the husband's stress. She wants to work, and I'm told you received a promotion at Castle Builders recently."

"I'm now front desk manager for day and night shifts," Catherine proudly announced. "We're looking for a part-time morning secretary. How is Sandra with answering phones?"

"She'll do quite well with the right opportunity," he offered.

"And how does the Janet Network do this sort of undercover operation?" Catherine questioned. "What do I do? Just walk up to her and ask if she's looking for a job and that Castle Builders is hiring?"

"Leave the job introduction to me," he said.

She walked over to him and smiled. "You are the boss."

"So can I count on you?"

She nodded yes. "How can any woman refuse a request after you save her life?"

"None have. So far," he said with a smug grin.

"It's good to know that you are giving their marriage another chance."

"As long as he's willing to try, I won't give up on him. I do, however, worry about Sandra's self-esteem. Having a job and a steady income will help her tremendously. It will also give her a chance to be a little more independent. That, along with Arnie's anger management, may save their 26-year marriage," he said hopefully.

She walked over to him and began straightening his long white tie underneath his white wing collar. Her hands ran over his black peak-lapel cutaway jacket to brush off the shoulders. "You look incredible today!" she concluded, her hands stopping on his silver initialed cufflinks. "Stanley must be very happy I got you in this tuxedo."

"I surprised him this morning with tickets and he's making arrangements with his work," the doctor announced. "He's picking me up at the reception and then we're off to Miami for a nine-day cruise to the islands."

Suddenly a knock sounded on the door.

Catherine gasped, grabbing the doctor's arm. "It's time!"

The doctor opened the door and together they walked out. "By the way," he said, so low she could hardly hear it, "I've never seen a woman so beautiful."

CHAPTER 52

When they arrived at the front of the church, Jay kissed Catherine on the cheek. They stood at the bottom of three stairs which led to an altar where the minister stood holding a white Bible with gold trim.

"Who gives Catherine to this man, Will Cilva, for holy matrimony?"

"Jay Newport." He walked her up the stairs and gave her hand to Will.

Jay retreated and stood beside the last of the groomsmen.

"Do you, William Cilva, take Catherine to be your lawfully wedded wife, to have and to hold from this day forward, for better and for worse, for richer and poorer, in sickness and in health, for as long as you both shall live?" The minister glanced up at Will.

"I do," he said, proudly.

"Do you, Catherine Walters, take Will to be your lawfully wedded husband, to have and to hold from this day forward, for better and for worse, for richer and poorer, in sickness and in health, for as long as you both shall live?" He then looked at Catherine.

"I do," she replied, smiling.

"At this time, Catherine and Will have their own messages to convey to each other." The minister closed his Bible. "Catharine, you may begin."

"Will," Catherine's eyes welled, "you have been my rock through the worst times of my life. You never gave up on me. You trusted me to make the right decisions and you showed me a real man doesn't need to exert control over others but be in control of his feelings and his heart. When I grew into the woman I am today, I looked inside myself to really know what kind of man I want to spend the rest of my life with. That man, one who is kind, passionate, honest and loyal, is you. I could never love a man more. We have grown so close as a couple that I can't even imagine my life without you now. We've been through the worst of times. I am honored to have you as my husband, and I want you to be proud of making me your wife."

Will suddenly choked up, but he finally responded. "From the moment I first laid eyes on you, I thought we'd make the perfect match. I saw what I see before me today, a woman with a soul bigger than she is. You're the one who changed me for the better. You made me grow into the man I've always wanted to be. I promise you, from this day forward, I will always be proud to have you in my life. I will show you every day how wonderful it is to have you, Catherine, in my life forever."

The minister raised his hands. "For the glory of God, in honor of the love he has shown this couple, let them exchange rings in the bonds of matrimony." Will picked two rings off of a pillow held by his ten-year-old nephew, the ring bearer.

"Will, repeat after me," the minister said. "With this ring, I thee wed."

"With this ring, I thee wed." Will placed a diamond ring on the fourth finger of Catherine's left hand.

"Catherine, repeat after me." The minister repeated the phrase.

Catherine placed the ring on Will's fourth finger of his left hand. "Will, with this ring, I thee wed."

"What God has joined together, let no man put asunder," the minister said. "You may kiss your bride, Will." Will took a step forward, leaned over and kissed Catherine deeply on the lips as the crowd began to cheer.

"It is with great pleasure that I introduce to you Mr. and Mrs. Will Cilva!" The minister clapped along.

Music began to play. Will released Catherine from the kiss and gave her his arm. Together, they moved down the center aisle on a petal strewn path and across the hallway to the fellowship hall, where everyone joined them for the reception. Soon, the celebration piled out through the large glass doors onto the large terrace where the wedding party and guests enjoyed a view of the beautiful church gardens. Tables were set up on the terrace, part of which served as a dance floor. On each table was a large vase of red roses, white plates with red rose trim and silverware. A small orchestra played nearby.

Suddenly, Will lifted Catherine up in his arms, hugged her tightly, and wildly spun her while photographers quickly took their picture. Servers carried plates of caviar with crackers, shrimp cocktails, crab cakes, broccoli cheese puffs and mini quiches among the guests. The crowd began to disperse, finding their tables among the many blooming flowers. Shaking hands and giving hugs to friends and family, Will and Catherine began to greet their guests at each table.

When they approached the doctor, Catherine noticed that Dr. Newport had seated himself at Sandra's table which was not where she had placed him. She had originally had his seating near Will's head table. Beside him sat Margie, his secretary, and Stacey from the Employment Office who had helped Catherine get the job at Castle Builders.

Catherine smiled. "Thank you for the walk down the aisle, Doc."

"You're welcome." He raised his champagne glass.

"So, is it true?" Stacey asked. "I heard from your aunt you're the new desk manager at Castle Builders. That is quite an opportunity for you to grow with the company." Stacey turned her attention to Will. "You must be very proud of your new wife."

"Oh, I am, but with her promotion, they will need to hire a part time secretary for the morning hours. Catherine will be working during the afternoon and early evening," Will added.

"The pay is twenty an hour and the hours are somewhat flexible, so it shouldn't be a hard position to fill." Catherine tried hard not to notice Sandra was very interested.

"How coincidental," Sandra said. "The good doctor was just telling me I should start looking for employment, and this job sounds perfect for me."

"Catherine, do you know Sandra," the doctor queried surreptitiously.

"I do!" Catherine exclaimed. "She's one of my new relatives!" Her attention turned to Sandra. "Why don't you come into the office, and fill out an application."

The enthusiasm on Sandra's face was almost palpable. "I type very well, and Arnie and I could really use the extra income right now."

"Sounds perfect." Catherine smiled.

"Who is in charge of Human Resources for Castle Builders now that Janet's gone?" the doctor asked.

"I'll speak to my boss and see if I can conduct the interview myself first thing when I get back from our honeymoon," Catherine suggested. "I don't see why he wouldn't agree."

Stacey suddenly started fanning herself with her large napkin. "Is it hot today?" She shot a quick look at the doctor and then her eyes returned to Catherine. "Hot, Catherine?"

"Yes." Margie giggled. "Hot Stuff, out here today. Wouldn't you say, Catherine?"

Catherine knew they were referring to how the doctor appeared in a tuxedo, not the temperature. "Really, are you both hot?"

Oblivious to their compliments, the doctor straightened his jacket. "I don't find it warm."

"Oh, it's hot." Stacey winked at Catherine. "Very, very, hot stuff. Wouldn't you agree with us, Catherine?"

Catherine returned the wink. "Too hot to handle, that's for sure."

She and Will moved on to the next table to greet more of their guests. "You think Sandra will apply for the job?" Catherine asked, once they were out of Sandra's ear shot.

"Of course." Will wrapped his arm around her.

"It's nice to know we can help her."

"You learn fast." Will smiled down at her. "Welcome to the Janet Network, Mrs. Cilva."

CHAPTER 53

They danced around the terrace to their first song as a married couple, clinging to one another, so in love. "This is the happiest day of my life," Catherine whispered softly in Will's ear.

He tightened the embrace as the song faded. "This is only the beginning," he promised.

While everyone applauded, the orchestra leader tapped the bride on the shoulder. "Mrs. Cilva now is typically where I play the father-daughter song. If you would like I could ask the gentleman who walked you down the aisle." He pointed to Doctor Newport who was still talking with Sandra at her table.

"What do you think, Will?" Catherine asked him. "Would you mind if I danced with Doc?"

"Of course not." He smiled, then added to the band leader, "Go ask Jay if he wouldn't mind."

"All right, I'll ask him." He headed over to the table as Will escorted Catherine to the middle of the dance floor.

As he spoke to the doctor, Catherine watched his big blue eyes immediately trail to hers and, with the smile moving across his face, she knew what the doctor's answer was.

"Looks like I've got my next dance partner."

"Just as long as you save the rest for me." Will gave her a quick peck on the lips and stepped away. As the doctor approached, Catherine watched him pull the rose from his lapel. They met in the center of the dance floor and the doctor's face suddenly lost its smile.

"Ladies and Gentlemen, in honor of Catherine, Dr. Jay Newport has requested a tango instead of the father-daughter dance," the director announced over his microphone.

Catherine's eyes widened in shock.

"You'll do fine." The doctor stuck the rose behind one of Catherine's ears.

"I haven't done the tango since high school dance class," she stammered. "I'm not sure I remember all the steps."

"It's not about remembering all the steps. The tango is my favorite of all dances. Do you know why?" The doctor raised his arms shoulder length for her hands to lift to his. "It's a dance of endearment and you are very dear to me."

"It requires two to feel that way." Catherine grinned. "And I certainly do."

The doctor waited for the music and then began leading her in a straight line. He varied the path. In a whirlwind of syncopated movements pivoting toward the left, he and Catherine tangoed across the floor. He adjusted his grip and then twirled her around, keeping his head up in a perfect leading stance.

Catherine was spellbound by their dance embrace. Captivated by the music, she let him guide her, enjoying the feel of his arm around her back.

"Perfect," the doctor complimented. "Now show me the woman you have become, one in control of her own destiny."

Catherine broke away and began twirling her white skirt to the beat of the music. She circled him until he captured her once again in his arms. With the last three beats of the music, he dropped her back, leaning over her as if to kiss her lips.

Instead, she grabbed the rose out of her hair and stuck it in his mouth. With that, she stood, taking a quick bow as the crowd stood, clapping. The doctor bowed alone for a moment, until she went back to him, removed the rose from his lips, and planted a kiss upon his cheek.

"I'm very happy for both you and Will." The doctor's smile beamed. "Will is a good man. He'll treat you very well. And now I must say good night."

Instead of heading back to the table where Sandra and Arnie were seated, the doctor stepped down off the veranda and headed out through the gardens. Catherine's eyes followed him out to his black sports car parked on the street. The convertible top was being lowered and Stanley sat in the driver's seat. He raised a hand in greeting to her and she responded in kind as several of the female wedding guests began surrounding Catherine with their own inquiries.

"Who is that?" one asked.

"Isn't he gorgeous?" another commented.

"I heard he was a doctor," one woman added.

As another song began and those on the floor began to dance, Catherine continued to watch the doctor as he climbed into the passenger's side of the car.

Will strode up and wrapped his arm around his wife. He and the doctor exchanged waves as the sports car pulled away from the curb. "Mrs. Cilva…" He pulled his wife close to his side. "I don't believe I have ever seen such a sensual tango. Should I be jealous?"

The doctor's car drove away, and Catherine returned her gaze to the man who had not only saved her life but had changed it for the better. Completely happy, she felt like she was an entirely different person than the one who had been with Lucky. She smiled. "Don't worry. My tango days with the doctor are over. It's time I enjoy the rest of my life being married to the man who loves me."

"What's not to love? You're gorgeous, sexy and intelligent enough to marry me, right?" He chuckled.

"Yes." Catherine kissed Will passionately. "What's not to love about me? I finally started believing that and it's made all the difference in the world."

Epilogue

Jay walked into his office and glanced at the woman sitting on the sofa opposite his desk. He didn't recognize her at first. Then her head rose and from underneath a big red hat he immediately recognized the attractive diminutive features.

"Abby?" He placed the file he was carrying on his desk.

"You put your name down on the register as Shelley Parker."

"Sorry to lie about my identity, Doctor Newport. I didn't know how else to see you except to pretend to be a new patient."

Towering over her, he realized, "You're a blonde now?"

"I've always wanted to be a blonde. Red just wasn't me."

"What can I do for you, Abby?" he asked, suspiciously.

"My brother Lucky is going to jail for a very long time," she said coldly. "Catherine and you must be very proud of all your hard work."

"Why have you come here, Abby? I take it you aren't interested in my services as a doctor."

Laughing, she got up from the sofa, her thin frame adorned in a tight, red dress that showed her cleavage and her long, shapely legs. Slowly, she headed for the door without looking him in the eye. "No good deed goes unpunished, freak."

"Abby? Are you threatening me?"

Her eyes went to his. At first, they appeared soft, almost affectionate until a coldness glazed over. "You'll both pay for what you did to my family," she promised matter-of-factly.

"There's no need for revenge." The doctor placed a hand on her shoulder. "My problem was with Lucky."

"Didn't you think for one moment how it would affect me? Lucky was all I had in this whole world! Catherine is nothing but a whore and you helped her put my brother behind bars for life."

"Stop it!" The doctor tightened his grip. "Catherine didn't even know what your brother was into. He was the one helping the Millers sell drugs, not her. Lucky deserves to be in jail, and she did nothing wrong."

Abby suddenly smiled. "Still protecting her?"

"Are you planning on hurting Catherine? Because if you are, you should know the DEA already had Lucky under surveillance before we ever learned of Lucky's drug trafficking. You can't blame us for your brother's criminal activities."

"You're right." Her smile dropped. "I can't blame you for that. I can, however, find fault that you both are the reasons he got caught."

"Please have a seat, Abby." He pointed back to the sofa. "Let's talk calmly about this and maybe I can get you to a counseling service that can help you deal with your brother going to prison. It was thoughtless of me not to have considered how tragic this would be for you. I know how much you love your brother."

Abby's eyes filled with tears.

"Come and sit." The doctor stepped toward his desk. He pressed the button to alert Margie to contact the police department. He realized he needed only a few minutes to keep Abby there. "I should apologize for your grief."

"You think saying your sorry is going to change what happened? Is that going to set my brother free?"

"He's not dead," the doctor reminded her. "You can visit him."

"Is that supposed to make me feel better? Catherine and you destroyed my life and my brother's!" Abby slapped his face. The hit was so loud, the doctor could hear Margie gasping right behind the door.

A knock came.

"Margie, I'm fine." The doctor removed his glasses and rubbed his cheek. "Just show our guests in when they arrive."

"You called the police," Abby guessed. "Smart, but I haven't done anything yet."

"Assault is a crime," the doctor finished, touching his face. "Although, if you leave now, I won't mention it."

"I'll go for now." Abby walked over and grabbed the doorknob.

"Rest assured I'll be taking out a restraining order and telling Catherine to do the same," the doctor warned her. "I won't stand for threats from you, Abby, especially against Catherine. You need help. Counseling may do you some good. I want you to look into it."

"Sweet, precious Catherine." Abby rolled her eyes and added sarcastically, "Would I hurt the woman who promised to love my brother forever? She's so honest, isn't she?"

"Is that another threat?"

"No, but this is. Your Janet Network is through, Doctor!"

Police sirens could be heard through the open window. The doctor looked back and heard the door opening. Abby rushed out of his office, through the waiting room and into the parking lot.

The doctor told Margie at her desk, "Call Catherine. Tell her I need to see her immediately."

Margie rushed over to him, studying his face. "Your cheek is bright red.

Are you okay?"

"For now. I have a feeling though. This isn't over by a long shot." He took in a deep breath. "I want to see Catherine as soon as possible and let the police in."

"Yes, Doctor Newport." Margie's eyes widened in fear as she hurried toward the phone to make the call.

ABOUT THE AUTHOR

Michele Wallace Campanelli is an American writer, singer and Florida celebrity. During the early 1990s, Michele was lead singer of the heavy metal band, Black Widow, which was one of the first all-female bands in Florida during the early 90s. Her nickname was Screech. After the band, Michele Wallace Campanelli started writing short stories and fiction novels professionally. She has had nine stories appearing on the best-sellers list, including two that reached #1 on the New York Times. Her short stories have been included in over 30 international selling anthologies. She has also penned numerous novels, magazine and newspaper articles in both fiction and non-fiction published by Simon & Schuster, Chronicle Books, Fireside Books, Whiskey Creek Press, Wee Creek Press, Fictionwise, Florida Today Newspaper, Woman's World Magazine, Adamsmedia, McGraw-Hill, Multnomah Books, Red Rock Press, HCI and America House Publishing. Over 57 million people have read her written works internationally. When Michele isn't writing, she is CEO of Regal PA & Entertainment Services LLC which performs concerts around Central Florida. She is a professional singer, writer and actor. As a devoted Christian, she uses her talents to glorify God and bring joy to others through music and her books.